AF224077

Ray Anthony was born in Kingston Jamaica in 1958 and lived with his grandparents until 1968, when he came to Britain to join his parents. Educated in south London, when he had the choice, he studied only maths and science - he found the arts crushingly boring. His first employment was in retail management, then he joined the Royal Air Force. After leaving the Royal Air Force he changed career to media sales management. It was during this time that he discovered he had a hidden creative bent. *'Less of my time was being spent on selling or managing, and more on shuffling pieces of paper. Writing strategic reports did my brain in, so I started 'jazzing them up'. The bosses were not amused. If I wanted to keep my job and my sanity, I had to find some release.'* In 1987 he started writing his first novel. He is now a media sales consultant and finds that training salespeople gives him ample scope to exercise his theatrical predisposition.

Also by Ray Anthony

Science Fiction
Pilot
Empress

Contemporary Fiction
All Woman
Interface

Non Fiction Humour
Thinking Man's Guide To Pregnancy, Childbirth &
Fatherhood

INTERDICTOR

The Unknowable Enemy

Book One

Ray Anthony

ACE - London

Copyright © Ray Anthony 2015

All rights reserved
No part of this publication may be reproduced, stored in a retrieval
system, or transmitted, in any form or by any means without prior
permission in writing of the publisher, nor be otherwise circulated in any
form of binding or cover other than that in which it is published and
without a similar condition including this condition being imposed on the
subsequent purchaser.

ISBN 978 1 8382975 1 0

PO Box 10289
London SW17 9ZF

www.acebooksonline.com

Chapter 1

The noise of the engines in the enormous hanger was deafening. Yet above the roar of the Hoppers, as they streamed in through the space doors, was the low-level, agonising moans of thousands of casualties. The battle cruiser *Ostal's* main hanger had, over the last twenty minutes or so, taken on the guise of an enormous, frenetic, and utterly chaotic triage area. Hoppers hovered, seeking a footprint of unoccupied hanger floor, landed, unloaded the dead and the dying then took off again. Amid the mass of bloody and charred combat-suited human forms the semi-intelligent battlefield medical units vied with automated stretcher-bearers, floating blood banks, medics, and doctors to 'identify and prioritise'.

Among the hundreds of medical personnel Lieutenant Commander Katrin Rebora and a combat medic were kneeling, working intently on a badly burnt soldier whose combat fatigues were still smoking.

"Sedate, tag for icing," Katrin instructed then, with aching limbs, stood. She looked around at the sea of bodies then quickly moved to another casualty being attended to by another medic. Peaking over the medic's shoulder, she took an instrument from her pocket and pointed it at the casualty.

"Tracheotomy. Sterilise. AB positive. One litre," Katrin said to no one in particular.

A blood bank drifted over and hovered above her and the medic. They responded like a well-drilled team: putting away the instrument Katrin raised both hands towards the bank which scanned then sprayed them. As soon as this was done the medic reached up got his hands scanned and sprayed then detached a drip from the blood bank. With the casualty's arms mere blackened stumps, he inserted the drip into a vein in the casualty's leg.

Dropping to her knees Katrin wearily muttered, "Hundred-and fifty-watt scalpel."

The medic took a laser scalpel from the blood bank's tray and slapped it into her outstretched hand. Katrin stooped and without ceremony started to operate on the casualty's neck. The casualty, a just-out-of-school eighteen-year-old, remained conscious throughout but like a hardened veteran didn't utter a sound.

A kilometre away in a far corner of the hanger, a petite marine wearing an immaculate dress uniform, incongruous amongst the surrounding carnage, entered the hanger. Appearing to be even more youthful than the casualty, she took in the vista with one dispassionate sweep. Then daintily and fastidiously taking her time to step around the blood, guts, and disarray she made her way unerringly over to stand behind Katrin.

Stretching while rising from the floor, Katrin handed the scalpel back to the medic. "Dress. Tag, Bag. Rehab."

As she was about to move to another casualty, the marine tapped her on the shoulder. "Lieutenant Commander Rebora, I'm Colonel Novalta. We have a priority on a bioprep."

Katrin turned, made as if to protest then changed her mind. Again, she raised both hands to the blood bank. "Excoriate and sterilise." As the bank scanned her hands the surgical gloves she had been wearing started to evaporate. Then the bank sprayed and dried her hands. Both women made their way purposefully out through the chaos.

"Bioprep? Colonel, I know you combat types are immune to suffering and are probably unaware that the medical units can't really hack it, plus there *is* a shortage of doctors..." Katrin left it at that.

The Colonel smiled. "It's Mary... You medical types, despite the patent evidence, are probably unaware that we've been on the wrong end of a one-sided beating and need to do something about that - it's a combat thing."

Having been yanked out of medical school, tossed into a uniform, given some inane rank and been told 'she was now in *The Navy*' one of the first, and most painful, lessons she'd learned was 'orders were orders.' *Bloody military!*

***

The isolation unit was a four-metre square space crammed with LCDs, automation and hi-tech medical apparatus that was also bathed in red light. In the centre of the unit was a bed. Lying asleep on it was the Platinum Stinger Lume, a tall, lithe, sweet looking man. His wrists were handcuffed to the sides of the bed by electronic manacles. Mary and Katrin entered the room via a door which opened like an iris dilating. The door contracted behind them with a hiss. They stopped a metre from the bed to look down at Lume. As Katrin started to move closer Mary flicked out a hand across Katrin, blocking her path and continued to examine him. Satisfied that he was asleep, Mary lowered her hand.

Annoyed, Katrin moved to manipulate a console by the foot of the bed then, making a point, remained by the equipment. Keeping her eyes on Lume, Mary reached out, grabbed Katrin by the back of the collar and pulled her away from the bed.

"What's your problem, he's handcuffed. What's he done?

Mary gave her a scolding glance then refocused on Lume. "Feet."

"What?"

"His feet aren't restrained."

"So?"

"That's a Platinum Stinger, Doctor."

Blinking, Lume gradually awakened. His eyes, iris and cornea, were coloured jet black. He slowly and deliberately scanned the entire unit, eyes finally coming to rest on the two women. He raised an eyebrow then smiled. "Infra-red?"

"You're being prepped for a leave-behind," Mary informed him.

Lume tried to move his arms, couldn't and looked down at the handcuffs. "Shackles?"

Mary regarded him impassively "I am Colonel Novalta, your briefing officer and this is Lieutenant Commander Rebora, the medical transition supervisor."

With an icy calmness he stared at each woman in turn. "Shackles."

Fists clenched, he wrestled for a few moments against the restraints then gave up. All the while Katrin stared lustfully at him.

"A tactical withdrawal is under way, so your deployment has been moved up." Mary ignored his protest.

With subdued anger Lume glared at Mary. "Shackles!"

With obvious excitement Katrin read the console then piped up, "It's a low oxygen atmosphere. As the germ-lines take there will be hormonal imbalances that may have a significant effect on your behaviour..."

"Your lungs will adapt within twelve hours at which point your testosterone levels will be normal. Until then, sex drive-wise..." With a blasé shrug, Mary left it at that.

Lume took a moment to consider the implications of this. "So, the plan was to have me on ice until I was prepped... Just how *tactical* is this withdrawal?"

"You've been under for twenty-nine hours - the eyes take longest. Prepping and briefing will be concurrent," Mary continued business-like.

"That tactical." Lume seemed highly amused then became more sombre, "Losses?"

"You don't want to know," Mary answered, equally sombrely.

"So really tactical then. It seems like I only got back this morning from another crop-dusting."

"There're some of us who'd feel privileged to be selected for a leave-behind."

Lume disdainfully looked the diminutive Mary over, from her feet to the top of her head. "A leave-behind is a Stinger's errand."

Frostily, Mary stared back. "Re: your over-active glands, do I have your word?"

Lume stared at Mary for a long moment, then... "You have my word."

Mary reached for a device on her belt and the handcuffs snapped open. Katrin took an involuntary step backwards. Lume sat up, sniggering at Katrin, while distractedly massaging his wrists. "Omega Zero Three?"

Katrin raised an inquisitive and expectant eyebrow as Mary asked, "Yes, how did you know?"

"Low oxygen, low light. Never been prepped for infra-red before..." He stared at Katrin then grinned wickedly. "...didn't realise that you could see fear."

Katrin defiantly stepped back up to the console.

"You're on board the battle cruiser *Ostal*, over the next four to five hours you will begin to find the atmosphere on board too oxygen rich. The percentage and partial pressure in here will be fine." Mary indicated a pair of darken goggles by the side of the bed. "R & R until then."

***

One of *Ostal's* many canteens was abuzz with the general chatter of several hundred enlisted personnel: a broad mixture of races and ethnicity. All were dressed in combat greens and most of them were walking wounded. A group of seven scruffy looking male and female soldiers, having finished their meal, collectively rose from their table and tiredly started making their way through the crowd out of the canteen. One of the female soldiers, Sergeant Khan, stopped for a moment and held her hand to her earpiece then caught up with her comrades.

"They've finally allotted us a berth somewhere down on deck seventeen 17, grab the kit and decamp there. I'll go check the suits."

One of the soldiers grumbled, "Let's hope it's more salubrious than a week of kipping in a corridor."

Sergeant Khan grimaced. "Be thankful for small mercies, JJ. I hear that on some ships it's been standing room only for over a week. Be pretty smartish about storing the kit, we'll jump soon. The extraction detail must be about done."

Another of the soldier snorted, "What's there to extract, Sarg? We got smeared over the face of that planet."

Khan shrugged as the group ambled out. The wide corridor outside the canteen was overflowing with dishevelled and dispirited soldiers trudging along, whilst in their midst some were sleeping on the floor or simply trying to find a space to bed down. As the seven soldiers made their way through the organised confusion, Sergeant Khan collected small disks from each of her comrades, placed them in her breast pocket then separated herself from the group and turned off down an adjacent corridor.

Spaceships were not designed with a surfeit of dead space, however, any passageway that led to a main magazine needed to be cavernous to facilitate the loading of the multitude of outsized munitions. High up on one of the gantries overlooking the corridor, Lume, wearing the darkened goggles, was perched, arms folded, calmly observing the horde below. He was dressed in a conspicuously different, completely black one-piece suit. Continuing the theme of understated exceptionality, the only ornamentation on the suit was the Platinum Stinger's insignia on its lapels.

Sergeant Khan continued to make her way down crammed corridors and gangways filled with soldiers and the stench of suffering. Moving deliberately, she gingerly stepped around, and over, the troops sprawled everywhere as if wading through a refugee camp. Then, she descended a series of stairs and ladders. The multitude and unmilitary disorder progressively thinned out at each level as she moved further into the bowels of the ship, finally arriving at a long, dark, silent corridor with a door marked Armoury 7 at its dead-end. She halted in front of the heavily armed guard at the door.

"Sergeant Khan, 23rd Marine drop division out of *The Jakarta*. I understand that our suits are stored here."

The guard waved his hand in the air and a holographic schematic appeared in front of him. He studied it for a few seconds then whistled ruefully. "Only eighteen survivors from a full assault division drop." He then looked the Sergeant over. "Juicy?"

"More than juicy, salivating... *The Jakarta*?" Khan answered thoroughly bored.

The guard refocused on the schematic then slowly shook his head. "*Cion, Jakarta, Mooneen, Stark* and *Taurus*, plus a bucketful of others so crippled that they had to leave the party... Retina scan."

Sergeant Khan stepped up to an interface in the door and the hologram in front of the guard flashed twice. "Level six. Aisle twenty-six. Row twelve." The guard stepped aside, the massive re-enforced door silently swung inwards and Sergeant Khan strolled in. The door closed with a muffled thump behind her.

Armoury 7, the size of a respectable warehouse, was dimly lit and stacked from floor to ceiling with mirror-shiny armoured combat suits and infantry hand weapons hanging from racks. Sergeant Khan boarded an open elevator which lifted her several levels then came to a smooth stop. She disembarked and started to navigate her way purposefully along the aisles, checking aisle numbers as she went. Turning down an aisle she came to a batch of hanging suits that were only patchily mirror-shiny, intact but obviously damaged. Taking the disks from her pocket, she selected one and attached it to the front of a suit. The disk started to glow.

"*Achikeobi, Joseph. Lance Corporal. Space Marine. Sierra, bravo, eight, zero, nine, one, five, five. Diagnostics: main power level, one hundred percent; auxiliary power level, one hundred percent; primary bio systems, non-functional - repairing; secondary bio systems, thirty-one percent functional - repairing; communications, all channels functioning. Self-repair, seventy-three-point five percent complete. Combat ready in T minus nine hours,*" the suit's external communicator reported.

Removing the disk, she turned her attention to the next suit. As she selected another disk and reached out to attach it Lume stepped out from between the suits about five metres further down the aisle.

Sergeant Khan nearly jumped out of her skin. Stepping away from the suits, she turned to fully face him. "Yes, Platinum Stinger?"

Lume folded his arms and took a while to respond. "At ease, Sergeant. A proposition."

Khan looked on suspiciously but remained silent.

"I'm being prepped for a leave-behind," he indicated the goggles. "So, it'll be some time until I next have the opportunity to have an encounter..."

"How did you get past the retina scan?!"

Lume shrugged modestly. Khan dropped the disks and, whipping out her long combat knife from her boot, went into a defensive crouch.

"Whoa! You haven't heard the proposition yet."

The sergeant shuffled from side to side uncertain whether to defend, attack, or simply turn and run.

Lume looked at her askance then smiled. "An entire brigade pinned down. Taking so much fire that the ground in and around their position was starting to roast. All of a sudden, the spanking stops. Any idea why?" He gave her a moment to consider. "Someone, a sergeant I think, which could only mean that *all* the officers were dead, started clamouring to be evacuated but, of course, comms were being swamped. Then, behold, as if by magic, a Hopper comes a-fluttering down." Looking up to the heavens he let her ponder that as well. "Hmm... Now, let's see, only a body with UV line-of-sight comms could have given a precise fix to the boys and girls up top. No fire suppression, but the Hopper makes it all the way down and plucks up said sergeant and her oddments. Still no fire suppression and still no incoming fire. They made it all the way back to orbit, apparently. Remarkable."

He strolled towards the sergeant. "You know the proposition."

Knife poised, Sergeant Khan took a defiant pace towards him, determined. Platinum Stinger or not she was definitely going to fight! Lume continued to swagger nonchalantly towards her. As he drew close, she circled, ready to strike. But Lume sauntered past her then looked back over his shoulder.

"You owe me your life and all I was after was some female relief."

Chapter 2

The isolation unit was again bathed in red light and a relaxed looking Lume was sitting in the lotus position on his bed, diligently studying a holographic topological map displayed in front of him. The goggles were back in their original position. He moved his hand and the orientation of the map changed. As he focused on this new aspect with almost hypnotic absorption, the door hissed open and he was illuminated by an expanding shaft of bright light. He shielded his eyes.

Katrin marched in all business-like, flanked by two armed guards. She took three paces then stopped abruptly. The guards stuttered to a halt by her side nervously fingering their weapons. The door contracted behind them cutting off the bright light. All three started taking very deep breaths. Lume turned lazily and, blinking rapidly, looked them over with disdain.

"There has been an incident and an official complaint," Katrin stated officiously but then started to pant.

With a disinterested flick of his head Lume went back to examining the hologram. Katrin took a further step towards the bed and stood there defiantly. The guards followed her, now even more nervous.

As if surprised to see them there she turned to them. "Dismissed."

The guards exchanged a glance behind her back then stared at her as if she were insane.

"You are dismissed!"

Reluctantly the guards backed away, their eyes never leaving Lume. As they approached the door it dilated and bright light again flooded the isolation unit. At the door, one guard turned and stepped out while the other, ready to draw his laser, covered him. Once outside, he covered his partner as he stepped out. The door contracted behind them and the bright light ceased. Ignoring Katrin, Lume continued to examine the hologram in detail.

"The preliminary investigation has concluded that no offence was actually committed." Pausing she took a couple of deep breaths. "The complaint has been withdrawn. However, there is some... bewilderment, as to how you bypassed the armoury's security and its armed guard." She sucked in another lungful of the hypoxic air and moved a couple of paces closer to the bed. "So, were you able to find... release?"

Without taking his eyes off the hologram Lume asked, "Masochism or something to boast to your friends about? Assuming you live to tell the tale, of course."

"What?"

Without looking up at Katrin he chuckled, "Release? I'm sure you can see my bio read-out from there. And I can feel you trembling from here."

"I'm not trembling!"

Finally, he looked up at her. She stared back evenly. "So, you like playing with fire? OK. Strip."

"What?"

He waved his hand and the hologram disappeared, then he slowly unfolded his legs from the lotus position. "Presumably you sent your protectors away for a reason. Or do you believe you could get to the door before I got to you?"

He knelt on the bed and watched as Katrin self-consciously started to undress, letting her clothing fall to the floor.

"So, which is it? Terror-sex or the big boast?"

Becoming more emboldened in taking off her garments, she grinned at him. "I don't think you'd really hurt me."

He raised an eyebrow, amused. "Really?"

"She only had a knife." Now more self-assured, she continued to undress teasingly...

"It wasn't the knife." He gave her a deadpan stare and she froze and gazed back at him.

"She was a first echelon combat Marine," he stated in the most conversational of tones.

Cage now seriously rattled she made a valiant, if totally unconvincing, attempt to hide behind indifference. "So?"

"The only way I was going to get a fuck was with her unconscious. Comatose sex is hardly sex, is it?" He paused for effect. "Now you, my good doctor..." He lunged with incredible speed and wrapped both hands around Katrin's neck before she was even aware that he'd moved. He yanked her off her feet, swung her in a heels over head arc over his shoulder and slammed her onto the bed. Rolling back, he ended up sitting on her, hands still firmly clamped around her neck. "...are very much cognisant."

Speechless with fright but trembling with desire, Katrin stared up at the face looking dispassionately down at her.

***

The domed-shaped battle simulation theatre was darkened to twilight levels. Lume, wearing a transparent breathing mask, and Mary were sitting side by side in reclined tele-sensor couches; both were focused on the projection area. Mid-air above them was a hologram of an all-chrome manual typewriter in a camouflage carrying case.

"I don't see the purpose of this keyboard."

"It's a self-contained writing device to record your observations on paper."

"I have seen examples of annotating on paper by hand. That would be more effective and also not restrict my mobility."

"We estimate that it would take you two to three months to become proficient in making those annotations. It was known as writing."

"Weight?"

Closing her eyes momentarily to mentally access her couch's internal memory Mary said, "Only one point three kilograms, but there will be four kilograms of moisture resistant, crease-proof paper. Although Omega Zero Three is only point eight Gs, we wouldn't recommend taking them with you on your recces."

The hologram changed to show a pair of up-to-the-wrist hands feeding paper, typing, and carriage return - how to use a typewriter.

"Got it."

"Have you decided on your primary projectile weapon?"

"The bow and arrows."

"Really? I would have gone for the cross-bow."

"That has a greater range, but it's heavier and has a lower rate of fire."

Mary sat up and swung her feet off the couch to face Lume. The hologram faded. "Questions?"

Lume folded his arms and continued to stare up at the projection area. "Off the record: how sure are you that I need to be clean?"

Mary looked down at him a while before answering. "They appear able to detect, from ridiculous distances, and zero in on *anything* with an electric current flowing in it. We're not sure at all."

"I've been able to lash more than a few when wired."

"You've always been at the sharp end and survived, that's why you're the leave-behind."

Lume sat up and swivelled to face Mary. "What I don't know I can't tell, right?"

"Off the record: big picture; we haven't walked away from *any* engagement with less than eighty plus percent casualties. The intelligence database is full of nothing but conjecture."

Lume smiled. "I'll see what I can uncover about our enigmatic enemy."

Mary angered. "The fleet jumps in an hour. You gave me your word!"

Lume stared back implacably for some time... "I covered them while they were pinned down. Called in Casivac. Covered them all the way up to orbit. I did everything except wipe their arses."

Mary sat back with a start. "Did you explain this?"

Lume stood and adjusted his breathing mask. "Of course."

Mary also stood and looked up at Lume, incredulous. "And she wouldn't open her legs?"

Lume shook his head then shrugged.

"Fucking Norms," Mary spat out disgusted.

As they both headed for the door Lume eyed Mary surreptitiously; only Stingers referred to the general population as 'Norms'.

***

Katrin, wearing only T-shirt and knickers, sat on her bed leaning against the wall in the corner of the dimly lit two-bunk cabin. Eyes closed she appeared self-satisfied despite holding an icepack against her jaw and the evidence of several large bruises on her arms and legs. With only two bunks the cabin was allocated to senor officers but with space always a premium, the cabin was crammed with mechanical and electrical medical equipment. Without warning the door's iris hissed opened, boosting the lighting significantly.

Mary, still in dress uniform, entered the cabin and stopped abruptly. Taking her time to thoroughly look around she wiped her fingertips across a surface then examined her fingertips, seemingly deeply offended by what she saw.

Katrin slammed the icepack down on the bed, revealing a bruise on the side of her jaw. She winced with the sudden movement. "What the hell are you doing in here? How did you get in?"

Mary haughtily surveyed the cabin then asked conversationally, "Tell me what you know about Stingers?"

Katrin made to shuffle off the bed, suffered more discomfort, and thought better of it. "Get out!"

Mary took one pace to stand over Katrin. "What do you know about Stingers?"

"Clinically diagnosed sociopathic sadists," Katrin spat out bitterly.

Mary smiled. "And?"

"Predominantly male, usually above average intelligence. They project a facade of charm and sophistication but are inhumanly amoral. And, of course, they get their rocks off inflicting pain." This time Katrin's answer was delivered with dripping sarcasm.

Mary backed off, grinning. Pausing to look down at the unoccupied bed, as if personally affronted by the untidiness and lack of symmetry she fastidiously rearranged the cover then sat opposite Katrin. Making herself comfortable, she crossed her legs. "Almost textbook, Katrin. But, as a doctor, what do you really know about Stingers?"

"What more is there to know except we... The military take these brutes and forge them into the ultimate weapon system.

They exclusively make up our special forces. And, of course, if we weren't at war, they would all be in secure mental institutions."

"Oh, there's lots more to know, Katrin. For instance, they're extremely rare in the general population. Also, Gold and Platinum Stinger are invariably well above average intelligence - geniuses actually. Another thing of note is that their training cost more and takes longer than that of a starship's pilot. We go to extraordinary lengths to ensure that this investment is realised."

"And the point of all this?"

Mary stared at a spot just above Katrin's head. "It would not be in anyone's interest to have the idea abroad that they are any less dangerous than their reputation suggests."

Katrin returned the icepack to her jaw with one hand and unconsciously started to massage her bruised upper arm with the other. "Meaning?"

Mary leant back on the bed hugging her knees. "They're far too valuable an asset to be executed for, say, the crime of murder. And that's what will happen if combat personnel do not eschew association."

"So?"

"Katrin, as a doctor, what would your diagnostic be of someone who gets... euphoric sexual excitement from a liaison with a clinically diagnosed sociopathic sadist?"

Katrin stared back but didn't answer. Mary deliberately, released her knees, uncrossed her legs, and lent slowly towards Katrin. "Whatever you're into, well, that's up to you. But you must not communicate the incident with Lume to anyone. That is an order."

Katrin put down the icepack and took her time to carefully bum-shuffled to the edge of the bed. Once there she leant toward Mary so that their heads were almost touching.

"Colonel, they call you 'Scary Mary' don't they. Well, *you* don't scare me."

Mary smiled at Katrin. "I'm not trying to scare you. Katrin, this is important. You know you're not that... unusual. This gets out and some airhead, male or female, wants to play when he's having an off day... they could end up very dead. So, keep it to yourself. OK?"

***

The Medical Centre's surgical suite was a hive of frantic activity. Scores of doctors and nurses sat at consoles, screens and hologram projectors manipulating controls or giving verbal instructions. *Ostal's* wards, rehabs, and medical cryogenics were being locked down and like anything surgical it was being done by remote. Katrin, still covered in bruised and flanked by a nurse on either side, also sat at a console surrounded by screens. Floating in front of them was a hologram of a horizontal transparent human body showing the internal organs. This medical trio were calm and relaxed, in marked contrast to the frenetic activity around them. They took their time, meticulously scrutinising various sections of the hologramic body under different magnifications.

Eventually Katrin said. "Despite the haste, all germ-lines have taken. Your respiratory system has stabilised to Omega Zero Three temperate. Ocular system fully modified to IR and your digestive system..."

"Lock down! Lock down! Jump in five minutes!" blared over the Tannoy.

"...Digestive system only adapted to Omega Zero Three's flora - keep off the fauna."

All the other medical personnel in the Medical Centre redoubled their efforts.

"Roger, a confirmed herbivore I'll be." Several kilometres from the surgical suite Lume was in the dimly lit, warehouse-sized torpedo room that was crammed with automated machinery for maintaining and manipulating a vast array of different types and sizes of missiles responded. Breathing mask on, dressed in a camouflage suit, and looking relaxed he was lying in a three-metre long torpedo that was opened along its vertical axis. He and his low-tech equipment were packed tightly into shapes cut-out in impact resistance foam.

"We haven't had time to run tests but posit that the new proteins your body is producing are still insufficient; take boosters, regularly, as briefed."

"Check, I'll be an avid pill-popper."

Are you mission ready, Platinum Stinger?

"Lock down! Lock down! Jump in three minutes!"

All medical personnel, except Katrin and her two nurses, started rushing out of the medical centre.

"Mission ready."

Katrin manipulated a set of controls and nodded to the nurses who both moved to another set of consoles a couple of metres away. She surreptitiously checked that both nurses were fully occupied then turned back to her console with malicious intent. After another quick check on the nurses she leant forward and whispered, "All I have to do is change one parameter and you'd die slowly, lungs burning, gasping for breath, drowning in your own body fluids and in absolute *agony*, you bastard!"

"Lock down! Lock down! Jump in two minutes!"

In the torpedo room, Lume's torpedo started to close. *"You loved it,"* was his laughing response.

Just as Katrin reached for the control her hand was pinned to the console's work surface. Mary stood over her.

"Grow the fuck up, Katrin," Mary uttered evenly, quietly and with menace. The much smaller woman then released her fierce grip and turned to the nurses. "Let's go!"

"Lock down! Lock down! Jump in ninety seconds!"

Mary, Katrin and the two nurses sprinted out into the deserted corridor.

"Lock down! Lock down! Jump in sixty seconds!"

Chapter 3

Against the starfield background about thirty very large spaceships were strung out in a loose drifting formation. Most of the ships showed signs of severe damage and some were even still venting atmosphere. Well over half seemed to be the abandoned corpses of former magnificent ships signified by gaping holes in their shells and the lack of navigation or porthole lights. Drifting with the formation was a vast, dense, slowly swirling cloud of smaller misshapen debris. A tiny speck was ejected from the rear of one ship then the missile accelerated away from the formation. Twelve of the ships in the disorderly fleet broke formation, pulsated brightly for several seconds then jumped to superlight and vanished.

***

The missile entered the atmosphere on the dayside crescent of the red planet and began to generate entry heat. Its outer ceramic shell glowed red then white-hot and it descended further. There was a shrieking sonic boom as it plunged further into the thicker atmosphere. After several minutes it began to decelerate and started to cool. The shell changed from white-hot, to red-hot, to a neutral grey. Then the ceramic casing cracked like glass, shattering to reveal a dull green, maroon, and brown camouflage casing. At five hundred metres, just as the missile was about to impact terminally into the ground, a parachute deployed abruptly retarding it. The missile drifted down and landed gently on the ground.

Midday on Omega Zero Three was comparable to twilight on Earth. This dim alien landscape from horizon to horizon was a barren rocky brick-red plateau punctuated by an occasional copse of dense, weirdly entangled trees with their enormous purple leaves, under a yellowish sky. A slight breeze kicked up small dust-devils of the rusty grainy soil.

The missile opened along its seam and Lume leapt out and, at a low crouch, sprinted, zigzagging to the nearest copse and dived in. He crawled through the alien undergrowth back to the edge of the copse and, from between the foliage, looked out. There was nothing moving just the breeze, missile, parachute, and alien vista. Hunkering down Lume kept to his vigil by the edge of the thicket and didn't move for over an hour.

As night-time approached Lume crawled out onto the tableland. Crouching low, he moved tactically, reconnoitring the circumference of a two-hundred metre area centred on the capsule. He took shelter in a hollow and waited a further ten minutes before making his way over to the missile to unpack his kit. It was almost pitch black as he carried the kit, slowly, carefully, and silently back to the copse then started crawling through the dense vegetation. He bumped into the tangled bulbous roots of a huge tree. Squeezing between the roots he moved into a tiny burrow and examined it by feel because even to his red and infra-red spectra eyes it was pitch black. Satisfied he dragged his kit in behind him and started to set-up his base of operations.

***

Each of the several hundred Jump Suites on *Ostal* had about 200 personnel seated in rows like, and as dark as, a cinema. Every individual was strapped firmly into their acceleration couch: each wore a face mask that was connected to the backs of couches. Katrin and Mary sat side by side with the two nurses either side of them... Everything blurred and shuddered for a few moments then all was still.

With the stillness came the sickness. Katrin, along with most of the occupants of the Jump Suite, started to vomit into her face mask. As the couch straps were automatically released Mary nimbly rose from her couch and started to assist the more lethargic Katrin. When Katrin eventually got up from her seat in the zero G, she and most of her comrades were still disorientated, some were still puking.

'*Biocontainment shielding up! Stand by for one G in five... four... three... two... one!*'

The lighting in the Jump Suite brightened and the artificial gravity was restored.

"*Lock down over. Jump medical teams to Sector nineteen, deck fourteen and Sector twenty-seven deck forty-three.*"

***

Having slept only fitfully, Lume crawled out of the den into the dim early morning intent on a quick recce before chow or ablutions. Reaching back into the den he pulled out the bow, as he reached in for the quiver and arrows there was a loud high-pitched warble. He froze as all around him the alien trees randomly started to be blown, with a percussive boom, high into the air like rockets being launched. Each tree showered the surroundings with falling earth before shattering mid-air and raining splinters. Lume grabbed his weapons and sprinted at a low crouch as the woodland around him erupted. He made it out onto the tableland, covered in dirt and wooden fragments. Zigzagging, he ran about a hundred metres and dived into a shallow depression.

He peaked over the edge and scanned the area, the copse was still being systematically destroyed. His eyes came to rest on where the capsule he'd arrived in ought to have been - it was no longer there. Midway between the woods and his location the ground suddenly erupted, like a geyser, throwing earth hundreds of metres into the air. A succession of haphazard eruptions followed, each one getting nearer to his position. Upending the quiver, he hurriedly picked up an arrow and examined its non-metallic tip. He then took up the bow and quickly examined it as the eruptions drew ever nearer. Starting with his breasts he patted all his pockets; nothing in them for the eruptions to be homing in on.

His little pit was now surrounded by eruptions with rock-strewn debris raining down. He pulled his combat knife out of his boot, looked at its metal blade, then flung it as hard as he could in one direction, jumped out of the crater and sprinted off in the opposite direction. He ran zigzagging and dived head-first into a recently evacuated crater. Cautiously he popped his head up. The eruptions gradually started moving towards where the knife had landed.

"Your direction finding is shit," he muttered to himself.

He could tell the instant the knife was hit as there was an all too familiar shimmering bright flash. In Omega Zero Three's diffused light the flash left afterimages of orange and purple on his red and infra-red spectra eyes, but he knew the true colour to be blue/white. He'd seen it often enough when a combat suited soldier, or parts of a combat suited soldier, simply exploded from the inside.

How had they zeroed in on his knife? Stupid question, how the hell did the 'Bulges' manage anything? He hadn't the faintest idea how they got that moniker as very few who'd seen one up close lived to tell the tale. Personally, whenever he'd seen one, he'd always thought of it as an enormous caterpillar. Lume stayed put, making the still hot crater his mother's womb, lover, and best friend as he scanned from horizon to horizon - nothing more to see.

Here was another thing to add to the burgeoning catalogue of the Bulge weirdness; rarely were they actually visible. As far as anyone could tell they didn't move about much or use projectiles or energy weapons, *but* they always managed to beat the living crap out of anything that went up against them. It was always the same; that ear-splitting warble (now he was clean and not wearing a combat suit he could certainly appreciate that it was ear-splitting). Then, arbitrarily, shit starts exploding in your vicinity. And if you were stupid enough to stay still then you, said vicinity and an expulsion became intimately conjoined.

Some technical types had speculated that they accomplished all this by warping spacetime. He didn't have an opinion on that, being satisfied with a more generic 'they just can'. But their direction finding was woeful, as if it took them time to focus precisely on any given target. Not that there was much comfort in that, they always got a fix in the end. This was why he was going get comfortable in his crater and stay exactly where he was for at least the next couple of hours.

*****

There were only mini dust devils for company. They only served to remind him just how thirsty he was. No enemy activity, movement, or anything which, as far as he was concerned, was simply fine and dandy. Lume decided it was time to check on his kit, tracking down the disappeared pod would wait for later. As he got to his feet he spotted over a slight hillock, about half a klick away, another small hillock except... It looked more like a hundred-metre-high garbage mound and was completely out of keeping with the surroundings. Through red and infra-red spectra eyes he examined the peculiar hill for several moments: he'd never seen, or heard about, anything like that. Some instinct told him that could be why he was here, on a God forsaken planet, orbiting a star situated in the middle of nowheresville, as the sole Stinger leave-behind.

Tempering his curiosity, he cautiously headed for the obliterated copse he's set up base in. Not much remained: writing machine, waterproof paper, most of his rations and medication looked like they had been thoroughly shredded. As always, with anything to do with the efficacy of Bulge weaponry, there wasn't a fragment bigger than a few centimetres. Thankfully, his water supply was intact and, of course, he still had his primitive weapons. He gathered his meagre supplies and headed for another copse a few hundred metres closer to the anomalous mound.

Having satisfied some basic human needs, he familiarised himself with the copse's geography and potential exit routes before starting detailed observation of the mound/hill/whatever-the-hell-it-was. He wouldn't have much daylight as a day on Omega Zero Three was only 17.5 hours. So, what was it that he was looking at? A hundred-metre-high lump of something, that was about the same dimensions at its base, like an untidy ill-defined pyramid. His eyes were telling him that the mound was an iridescent mauve, but he wasn't too certain about that because his somewhat hasty deployment had deprived him of the luxury of calibrating colours. There was no movement in and around the mound just an occasional wisp of smoke rising or a dim flash of what he guessed would be blue light.

Because he was near the equator of the planet, twilight arrived abruptly. This must have triggered something because for no apparent reason the mound seemed to simply dematerialise. A few seconds later it reformed as five distinct mounds of various sizes with wisps of smoke streaming between them. So inexplicable was this that it took him a few seconds to accept that he'd actually witnessed the dematerialisation and it wasn't his new-fangled eyes playing tricks on him. No, there really were now five mounds. An educated guess said that the volume of the five smaller mounds added up to the volume of the original. *Well at least Bulges seem to abide by basic physical laws.*

Just as abruptly twilight faded to night, but he could still easily make out the silhouettes of the mounds, so they were obviously radiating heat. He'd been lying there for the best part of the Omega Zero Three night. No activity, nothing. Just as he was considering moving off, the five mounds dematerialised. No, they didn't just disappear; first there was a momentary blurring, then the mounds were no longer there. *But* the blurriness remained. Into that blurriness three mounds reappeared and seemed to take on solid form. Like... like a defective hologram focusing.

It was going to take a great deal of patience but there had to be an underlying pattern to this. He cleared away a patch of earth about half a metre square, took up a stick and, under his breath, started counting.

***

Katrin was in the Medical Centre, with a nurse on either side, administering to patients via remotes. The fleet had jumped away from combat space, but the medical workload hadn't lessened. The best guesstimates were that only about thirty-two percent of the infantry made it back. The vast majority of those had been casualties of one sort or another. In the days since the jump she hadn't even been back to her cabin; taking only an occasional nap under her console. Again, she and her colleagues had been presented with another medical catastrophe. At least on the ships that took terminal hits the crew died pretty instantaneously.

"You need to accompany me to the Flag Ship."

She found Mary standing immediately behind her. In the midst of all this madness, the Colonel still looked parade ground spit 'n' polish.

'Clearly this woman has Obsessive Compulsive Disorder issues.' "Why?"

Mary smiled. "The appropriate reply is, 'Yes Ma'am."

"I can't just wander off and leave my patients."

"Quite right. I'll just inform the Admiral that you'll be along in your own sweet time, shall I? You have fifteen minutes to make the necessary arrangements and be at Hopper Bay 6."

Mary sauntered out of the Medical Centre and Katrin stared after her. *'No doubt about it, OCD.'*

Chapter 4

There were now hundreds of ⵌ marks in rows and columns taking up an increased area of cleared ground as Lume observed the mounds, marking each transformation in the ground with a stick. Wearily he stopped, spent some time examining his calculations then took up his bow and arrows and began to crawl deeper into the copse. Occasionally he stopped, got to his knees, looked back through the undergrowth at the mounds then continued the crawl towards his base.

Just as he was about to reach a distance where the mound would no longer be visible, he looked back and saw something that was worth seeing. Like toothpaste being squeezed out, a tubular shape had detached itself from one of the mounds. Assuming his eyes weren't deceiving him, this meant a Bulge had actually *detached* itself from a mound. He rushed back to his original position in time to see what looked like a sixty-metre long, two-metre high, iridescent mauve caterpillar make a rapid dash that covered about half a kilometre in seconds. Then it stopped... Then it was off again in a new direction.

Lume observed the caterpillar for a while as it zipped over differing distances followed by pauses of indeterminate lengths and erratic directional changes. It didn't move at a consistent rate but instead seemed to be propelled by a series of surges. Its motion was jerky, haphazard, stop/start. What was it doing?

Looking for him he supposed, not that it was anywhere near. He was pretty sure, well, as sure a one could be about anything to do with the Bulges, that if he kept still it wouldn't be able to locate him.

Tracking the caterpillar, its remarkable speed, nonsensical route... That's it! Random! He's definitely on to something here so again he took up a stick and started counting silently.

***

Mary stood waiting impatiently, arms folded, by the airlock to Hopper Bay 6 as Katrin came running along the corridor.

"Sorry I'm late."

Mary shrugged and turned to have her eyes scanned by the door's entry system. "Obviously, your admirable bedside manner." The door opened and Mary entered without a backward glance.

The Hopper Bay was the size of a very large hangar and had dozens of the 50-metre long, pilotless, 30-seater, crafts parked. Mary strolled up to the nearest Hopper, as she approached the door opened automatically. Without breaking stride, she entered and, ignoring Katrin following behind, sat, and started to strap herself in. "Destination *Pantheon...*"

As soon as Katrin stepped in the Hopper the door started closing, she dived into the nearest seat and hurriedly strapped in.

"...Launch when cleared."

"*Destination* Pantheon. *Clearance received. Launching.*"

As the Hopper exited the Bay both Katrin and Mary turned to the front screen, but it was blank. Exchanging momentarily puzzled expressions they refocused on the screen... No, the screen wasn't blank there was simply nothing, no stars or anything, out there to view. This was utterly ridiculous -

interstellar space was never empty, it was never totally dark - space was always filled with light. Because there was no sense of motion both sat back with a start as the ghostly shadow of an enormous ship drifted by. The journey lasted over fifteen minutes and they glimpsed dozens of other ships that were only revealed if the Hopper passed very close to them. It would appear that *Ostal* was inside a dense stellar nebula and part of a very large fleet consisting of possibly hundreds of ships - a fleet of ships in hiding.

Then they were inside another Hopper Bay.

"*Arrival* Pantheon *disembark.*"

As Katrin and Mary made their way to OpsCen it soon became evident that *Pantheon* was a much larger combat vessel than the battle cruiser *Ostal*. En route, they passed scores of personnel who were obviously relaxed and at a low state of combat readiness. From Mary's point of view this meant that nothing terribly interesting was going to be happening any time soon. And if there was nothing terribly interesting here then there was lots she could have been getting on with on-board *Ostal*.

At the OpsCen entrance they were waved through by the two armed sentries. No retina scan, no ID, just a smart salute and 'In you go Ma'am'. Neither Mary nor Katrin had been this close to the centre of fleet power before. They couldn't help a momentary pause to take it all in. The OpsCen was a thirty-metre diameter amphitheatre. In the very centre was an outward facing circle of eight couches and consoles. Facing them was a circle of sixteen couches and consoles. Around those were another five concentric rings of inward facing couches and consoles. All the couches were reclined so their occupants could comfortably look up at holographs projected above the seats. It was obvious that OpsCen was also an independent Jump Suite.

This space could easily accommodate over a hundred personnel but only a handful of people occupied it. Sitting side by side in the inner circle of couches and consoles was a woman of African extraction and man who was probably a Eurasian mix; two middle-aged battle-hardened veterans: Admiral of the Fleet Ezocaagbo Akobundu-Tan and Field Martial Laurent Hooper. There were six Staff Officers sat facing them in the outer circle.

Mary and Katrin marched up to the two Field Officers, halted smartly at the outer circle and, in unison, saluted precisely.

Field Martial Hooper brushed off their salute and waved them to a couch. "At ease, please take a seat."

Mary and Katrin moved towards vacant seats, the outer circle of couches rotated so that two vacant couches faced the Field Offices. Gingerly, Mary and Katrin sat in them but were clearly not at ease sitting in front of such senior officers. It was also extremely difficult to look alert, serious, and respectful when reposed.

"This informal briefing is classified Most Secret," Admiral Akobundu-Tan informed them as she tapped her console.

As both Mary and Katrin nodded in acknowledgement several holograms popped up in front of the two Field Officers.

Field Martial Hooper focused on a particular hologram. "Lieutenant Commander, to which school of thought do you subscribe?" he asked without taking his eyes off the hologram.

"Err, I've examined fragments of so-called enemy tissue, Sir. There is nothing there that would lead me to conclude that we're dealing with a life form."

Hooper smiled at Katrin. "Ha! A natural phenomenonist. And you Colonel?"

"There is clearly purpose to their actions, even if we can't follow their rationale, Sir."

The Admiral raised an eyebrow. "So, Colonel, you believe that we are confronted by intelligences. If so, why haven't we been able to, at least, partially glean that rationale or establish even the most rudimentary communication?"

Mary looked back stumped and didn't answer.

The Field Martial took up the thread. "Their ships, if we can call them that, appear, devastate our fleets and then are gone. If we manage to chip off an odd fleck, what do we find even at subatomic scales?"

A hologram of something looking like a lump of dull red rock appeared mid-air above them. The hologram then broke the rock into a series of higher magnifications.

The Admiral waved her hand at the hologram. "A random assortment of elements, the occasional alloy, but nothing that we'd call manufactured or artificial."

"Twenty-seven years of war, twenty-seven years of technological advance driven by human ingenuity. And still all we can manage against their ships is to, as the Admiral rightly says, knock off the odd fleck. Are you both convinced that we're not confronted by something far beyond our understanding?" Hooper challenged both women.

The hologram disappeared as Mary and Katrin exchanged nervous glances.

"We've been able to hold the line, Sir." Mary had had enough of this morbid defeatism.

Admiral Akobundu-Tan slowly and thoughtfully nodded in agreement before saying, "If retreating after every engagement and drawing them away from our solar systems is holding the line, then, that we have."

"Do you know why we're still in the game?" Hooper enquired as if the two junior officers might possibly have an answer.

Mary and Katrin look back nonplussed.

"Because they never destroy *everything*," he eventually enlightened them.

"Or capture and hold ground, or interdict supply lines or, in fact, do anything that would make a rat's arse bit of sense." The Admiral continued as if she and the Field Martial were a well-polished performance double act.

All the holograms faded, and Field Martial Hooper looked slightly pleased with himself. "But we do know this: we are dealing with intelligences."

"With due respect Sir, but how do we know this?" Katrin demanded with seething insolence.

A look passed between Akobundu-Tan and Hooper. Neither elephant could, just then, be bothered to squash the ant. Hooper very tolerantly said, "We accidentally uncovered that the intense bursts of UV emitted by their ships, or whatever they are, is a form of communications. Now, information theory states that the information content of any message is distinct from its meaning. The more complex the content, the more information conveyed."

Mary sat up excited. "Have we been able to decode this communication, Sir?"

"No. We're nowhere near understanding *what* they're saying but we're getting a feel of *how* they're saying it," the Admiral answered.

A hologram of a basic x-y graph appeared and expanded to fill most of the projection area. Three downward sloping coloured curves were plotted as the Admiral continued, "The boffins refer to human languages as ninth order Shannon entropy, that's the blue line. And as a comparison; killer whales' communication is fourth order, green. The enemy's communication is fifteenth order, red."

The Field Officers gave them time to absorb this before Hooper added, "So here we are, the most powerful military force in human history, hiding from some seriously complicated alien intelligences. And we are desperately in need of a touch more serendipity."

Mary and Katrin exchange puzzled, 'where is this going', looks.

The Admiral pondered for a moment then asked of Mary. "The Platinum Stinger on the leave-behind, Colonel, as a Stinger Ops Officer, what's your take on his extraordinary survival and success rate?"

"Of late I haven't put boots on the ground, so it's difficult for me to assess, Ma'am." Despite her best-efforts Mary couldn't mask the surliness in her answer.

"Don't want to be chained to a desk, ha Colonel? So, Ops are unimportant then?" An amused Staff Officer piped up from her left.

Mary suddenly felt deeply uncomfortable as Admiral of the Fleet Akobundu-Tan stared blankly at her. "His debriefing reports suggest that he views combat as more a sophisticated game rather than a life or death struggle," she quickly answered then added. "This attitude might give some insight, Ma'am."

The Field Martial consulted a panel to his right. "Lieutenant Commander, it says here he has rations and supplements to last eighteen days. How long could he survive after these are exhausted?"

"Less than twenty-four hours, Sir. But rations aren't the issue. His bioprep was incomplete; after about sixteen days the local environment will have a cumulative toxic effect. Nineteen days is the outside limit."

Looking grave Admiral Akobundu-Tan stared off into nothingness for a moment then said, "What we have to decide is the cost/benefit of his retrieval. The costs are easy to estimate: eighty percent losses. That's three hundred and forty-seven ships, circa a quarter of a million personnel and the real possibility of our military collapse."

"No individual could possibly be worth that!" Katrin spat out in alarm.

The Admiral smiled and with an unexpected amount of patience said, "Correct Lieutenant Commander, no individual is. However, we've already lost two battle groups and one point three million men trying to get to grips with the Omega Zero system."

As even Mary started to look dejected Hooper cryptically added, "After twenty-seven years the enemy finally seems to be putting down roots."

Above them a new hologram appeared showing a solar system with several Gas Giants in the outer system and five rocky planets in the inner system. The hologram zoomed in on the third rocky planet that could have been Mars' twin.

"We need to understand why. Also, logic would dictate that we ought to deny them that foothold," the Admiral said.

"We're clutching at straws here, but the Platinum Stinger might provide invaluable intelligence," Hooper continued the double act.

Mary sat up suddenly, bright and breezy. "A covert operation might be preferable to a full-scale assault in his retrieval, Sir."

"It's eminently preferable." For a moment Akobundu-Tan stared at Mary like a bitterly disappointed high-achieving, parent then said, "However, we've never been able to penetrate their defences with less than a battle group. And, as you know, we were only able to get him in by using non-electrical systems."

"Are we really on the point of defeat, Ma'am?" Katrin asked despondently.

"I remind you that this briefing is classified Most Secret." She gave both junior officers time to reflect on this then continued. "In terms of economics, resources and manpower, eighty-plus percent losses are unsustainable. So, the answer to your question Lieutenant Commander is, yes."

"If we don't stop them here, it won't be just another beating in the long line of defeats. It will be the beginning of the end of mankind," Hooper added for good measure.

Mary sprang to her feet. "May I lead the extraction team, Ma'am?"

"As you've said, you're a way off being combat sharp, Colonel," a second Staff Officer replied.

***

On the return trip to *Ostal* Katrin and Mary sat in contemplative silence. Both were overwhelmed by the weight of the information they'd been given, the enormity of the upcoming operation and the secrecy of it all. Eventually Katrin looked over at Mary.

"I'm finding it really difficult getting my head round this idea that they are creatures - an actual life form."

Mary glanced at Katrin. "You also finding it difficult to not boast?"

"Wha...?"

"The word is out about you and Lume and I know where that came from."

"Oh." Katrin smiled then shrugged.

"I wasn't joking about keeping your mouth shut."

Katrin stared at Mary for while then dismissed her with a flick of her head. "Well, what are you going to do about it, Colonel?"

"Predominantly male," Mary said without emotion then calmly undid her seat straps, eased out of her seat, and stood over the bigger woman. "And it's not inflicting the pain..." She turned up her collar and, stared down with her child-like features, revealing a Gold Stinger insignia. "...it's about engendering utter powerlessness." She placed her index finger on Katrin's lips and added, "Button it or *we* will have issues!"

Chapter 5

Lume, now looking slightly bedraggled, sat cross-legged under a tree inside the dense vegetation. He was carefully whetting the point of a long stick with a sharp stone. By his side was a pile of eleven similarly sharpened sticks. Taking great care to avoid cutting himself he finished sharpening the stick then carefully rose to check on the alien mound. Satisfied, he gathered up the sticks, his bow and arrows and started to make his way tactfully out of the copse away from the mound.

Once out on the tableland, he paced out a straight line away from the copse. Occasionally stopping and checking behind him. He planted a sharpened stick in the ground every time he stopped. By the time he'd finished there was a line of sticks roughly twenty-five metres apart for about three hundred metres. Lume then took a circuitous route to move half a kilometre away and went to ground to observe the area. After an hour or so of no visible activity he started collecting small boulders. Twenty-five metres from the last stick in the line he started stacking the boulders, while still occasionally checking over his shoulder. He stopped building the stack when it was about his height. Even in Omega Zero Three's reduced gravity, this construction took a couple of hours and he was near exhaustion by the end.

Lume made another sweep of the entire area then moved back to the edge of the copse. He took the bow and notched an arrow. He aimed over the copse towards the alien mound, fired, then dove for cover and settled in to observe. He cleared a patch of earth with one sweep of his arm and snatched up a twig, ready to make marks, and started counting under his breath.

Through his red and infra-red spectra eyes he watched as an alien caterpillar charged around the corner of the copse. Moving rapidly, with its erratic stop/start motion, it zipped along and in and out of the line of sticks. Now Lume was this much closer, he could make out that the caterpillar's behaviour was even more bizarre and unpredictable than he'd first imagined. It wasn't just a matter of stop/start, it was as if the caterpillar was crashing against and then ricocheting off some invisible object. For the first time he was fairly sure, eighty percent sure, that he was observing a living thing and not a machine. He made a mark on the ground and continued to count.

As the caterpillar drew close to the pile of stones they suddenly erupted in a huge explosion of hypersonic gravel. All that remained was a smouldering crater several metres wide. From the other side of the copse two more caterpillars joined the first and all three started zipping haphazardly across the tableland. Though covering huge distances very quickly and with no discernible coordination between the three they were obviously searching for something. After several minutes all three caterpillars started drifting, surging and disjointedly, but definitely, towards his hiding place.

Without warning eleven of the twelve planted sticks abruptly shattered into tiny fragments creating, for a moment, what looked like a line of eleven puffs of amethyst smoke. Then the clouds of extirpated wood gently drifted to the ground. Only the first stick in the line was left standing. Lume made another mark in the soil and stayed put. Next there was a huge explosion behind and to the left of him. The blast casually tossed him a few metres forward to the edge of the tree line.

Ears ringing, winded and disorientated he lay there, showered with shredded foliage and detritus. His instinct cautioned him to remain absolutely still. A few moments passed before there was another explosion, this time, from somewhere further away. Another two more boomed in quick succession from even further. He smiled. *Frustrated grunts shooting up the place.*

Without moving he checked himself for internal or external injuries. Apart from a burning sensation on his left jaw, which he assumed was a simple abrasion, he was unharmed. With the discipline and patience honed from over fifty combat missions he remained perfectly motionless and waited. After an estimated twenty minutes he slowly crawled back into the copse and returned to where he had been keeping watch.

Having identified the patch of earth he'd been inscribing; with utmost care he cleared the space of debris. Damn! Over half of his marks had been erased by the blasts. He stared at the surviving hastily etched marks for a while then shook his head. What he had been attempting to record, as accurately as possible, were time periods but without having a timepiece. But this looked like...? He closed his eyes, concentrating on mentally replaying something, and silently counted nodding in time. Opening his eyes, he looked down at his marks. Closing his eyes once more, he took a deep breath, beating out a time with his nods and counted to twenty-three. Opening his eyes, again he looked down at his marks. It couldn't be that simple!

Then again, why couldn't it be so simple that no one had ever dreamt of running a simulation? Sitting up he looked up at the sky; he'd discovered vital intelligence and needed to get out of here soonest.

***

Omega Zero Six was one of several nondescript gas giants orbiting the Omega Zero star. At 2.3 Jupiter masses and just over eight AUs from its parent star it was the largest planet in the system - an unremarkable planet orbiting an unexceptional star. In a flare of dazzling lights, hundreds of human ships materialised in orbit from hyper-space. Remaining in orbit for several minutes the ships drifted into two loose equal sized formations. Then one formation broke orbit to head purposefully towards the inner system at sub-light speed while the other formation tightened, became more symmetrical and orbited closer to the gas giant.

On an intercept course for the planet Omega Zero Three the human ships swept into the inner solar system accelerating to 0.75 light speed. In the hour and twenty-seven minutes it would take them to reach planet orbit the two hundred and thirty-five ships manoeuvred to form a cone formation. Sub-light engines at maximum, with a single heavy cruiser at its apex, the formation took on the semblance of a gargantuan supersonic shockwave against the blackness of space. Just as the human ship had passed two thirds distance to target and were initiating heavy deceleration, the enemy ships materialised a few hundred thousand kilometres ahead of them.

Over a hundred of the neon blue, several kilometres long, always changing shape, enemy ships, were there; no outburst of light to signify re-entry from the super-light, no energy discharges to conserve momentum - the super-sized enemy vessels had just appeared!

The human ships immediately opened fire with lasers and high-G missiles. It took a few more seconds to target and lock-on their superconducting railguns. Then the near vacuum of space between the opposing fleets was saturated with tens of thousands of fifteen kilos depleted uranium shells, travelling at 0.69 light speed, heading unerringly towards the neon blue ships. Lasers, high-G missiles, and depleted uranium shells made multiple hits on a host of enemy ships without causing significant damage. The enemy ship seemed not to retaliate: no beams or missiles emanating from them, but the lead human ships started to explode from the inside; either being totally eviscerated or sustaining crippling damage.

Every time an alien ship took multiple hits, it fragmented - like a plait spontaneously unwinding. For the briefest instant there were hundreds of thousands of columns, like a shoal of immense iridescent wriggling eels. Then some of the two-metre-thick, kilometres long columns faded to a dull red colour, became rigid, inert, and continued to fly apart. The remainder rapidly re-intertwined to form a new smaller vessel that immediately re-joined the fray.

Still decelerating towards their objective of Omega Zero Three with the alien vessels impeding their progress, and despite suffering considerable losses, the human fleet kept its cone formation. Against the blackness of the star splattered background the human fleet was a riot of colours: the constant eye-watering intense white - like mini suns - of the sub-light engines, decelerating the ships; the deep crimson streaks of missile launches and the pulsing indigo flashes of railgun salvos.

In comparison to this display of humans unleashing such stupendous power, the alien fleet was less spectacular. Beside the neon blueness, the not quite here-ness, the never a defined form and immense size, their ships were positively prosaic. Prosaic but fearsomely effective; no formation, no apparent order or logic to their manoeuvres but they were tearing great chunks out of the human fleet.

Still the humans and their continuously diminishing formation pressed on. Despite having suffered over forty percent attrition, over several hours of ferocious space combat, they forced back the gargantuan enemy ships until the battle was raging in orbit around the planet Omega Zero Three. The progression was little consolation; despite all this firepower, and each alien ship being considerably smaller, there still seemed to be same number of enemy ships.

With the backdrop of the half-moon crescent of the planet and, without any fanfare, more of the alien ships appeared. With no discernible formation or with any apparent coordination they attacked trying to break the human cone formation. More of the enemy ships continued to appear, tipping the numerical balance in their favour, and taking out dozens of the human ships. Space around the planet and its upper atmosphere, like a comprehensively disrupted asteroid belt, was littered with damaged and destroyed ships; human ships burning, deformed, venting atmosphere, and slowly spiralling in their death throes. The sole remains of the enemy's ships were the billions of haphazardly twisted two metres thick columns drifting like a slowly expanding fog of kilometres long rusted iron beams - such different technology.

More alien ships materialised, the humans were now outnumbered, out gunned, cut off and about to be annihilated...

In the midst of this melee a second formation of over two hundred human ships materialised, in a blinding cacophony of lights, from hyper-space. Each ship clearly pre-programmed with target information to opened fire with everything the instant they hit normal spacetime. This tactic was immediately impactful, scores of the alien ship instantly disentangled into individual columns. The active alien columns tried to re-interlace but were hit with concentrated overlapping laser fire causing the newly formed ship to burst apart again and again.

Twenty of the newly arrived human ships broke off and descended to low orbit. Once there, while still engaging the alien vessels with sustained fire, they launched hundreds of Hoppers and Ground Support Fighters into the atmosphere, then immediately re-joined the brutal space battle.

***

Propped up under a tree in a dense wood, bow and arrows on his lap Lume, dishevelled and exhausted, slept. A loud low rumble in the ground around him startled Lume awake, as the ground started to shake. Lume crawled swiftly through the tangled scrub and falling leaves. As he moved, the earthquake became more severe, pitching him around as trees started to topple. This was no time to be tactical, getting to his feet he staggered forward as swiftly as the dense brush allowed. He reached the edge of the wood and looked out onto the tableland.

The alien mound was stretching upwards, growing in height, becoming thinner as it did so and writhing like a surreal super worm. When it reached, what he'd guess to be about, a couple of kilometres tall it was about two metres wide. And if he wasn't going to doubt his sight or sanity then the alien mound had transformed into a vertical, incredibly long, alien caterpillar. In the distance he could see scores of other similar long thin wiggling alien shapes like giant sand eels waving.

The super extended alien caterpillar, changed colour from iridescent mauve to neon blue and, bizarrely, slowly started to rise erratically like gargantuan sea-serpent taking to the air. An area of several hundred metres centred on the caterpillar was affected by an apparent anti-gravity field. Dust, stones, scrub, Lume and anything not rooted got lifted as the caterpillar rose. For a few seconds he was flailing about in this detritus swimming in a sea of air. Then as the alien caterpillar began an erratic upwards acceleration everything suddenly fell back to earth.

Lume must have been over a hundred metres up and if he had the supple agility of a feline - from Earth - he supposed he'd have landed on his feet. Unfortunately, and despite his best endeavours at aerial gymnastics, he landed on his shoulder. He heard his collarbone snap before he felt the pain. And he was still being rained on by debris of varying size. Lying on his back waiting for the pain to subside he had little option but to stare up at the sky. From horizon to horizon there were tens, if no hundreds, of thousands of the super extended alien caterpillars rising erratically. They seemed to converge like a rope interlacing which then interlaced with other ropes until, incredibly, they formed one of the immense neon blue enemy ships. And as soon as a ship took shape it winked out of existence. This was the sort of thing where if he hadn't seen it with his own, red and infra-red spectra or otherwise, eyes, he would have found hard to believe.

***

High in the sky of Omega Zero Three, the Hoppers, escorted by Ground Support Fighters, started losing their re-entry heat. Extending their wings, the formations initiated violent evasive manoeuvres while still descending. At a height of ten thousand metres the Hoppers paused their evasive manoeuvres momentarily to eject successive pairs of mirror-shiny armour-suited troops who had various handheld weaponry strapped to their backs. Then the Hoppers went back to their high G combat manoeuvres.

As each trooper exited a Hopper, they extended their limbs, spread-eagled like a skydiver. Holding this posture, they exploited their limited manoeuvrability to the maximum, gliding from side to side as the ground rushed up towards them at terminal velocity. Despite the dodging and speed of their descent many of the mirror-shiny armour-suited troops suddenly and inexplicably shattered into myriad pieces during the descent.

At a height of barely a hundred metres, each trooper's rate of descent abruptly slowed as the combat suit anti-gravity kicked in. They landed running, moving much faster than any unaided human can sprint, they drew their weapons from their backs then checked left and right for comrades who had also landed. Running in an extended line, spaced out at intervals of approximately a hundred metres they began their sweep. Planet-wide, well drilled squads of about thirty troopers, commenced predetermined search patterns initiating the difficult task of finding and retrieving a single individual who was electronically clean.

Up in the atmosphere high above the squads, without any sound or commotion, alien ships materialised. They immediately fragmented into thousands of the kilometre-long wiggling neon blue columns and started their erratic descent. Some took multiple laser hits from above, changed to a dull red colour, became rigid and fell like stones. With the vastly outnumbered Ground Support Fighters racing up to meet them most of the columns, raining down like falling chaff, were unaffected by this sporadic downward laser fire.

Chapter 6

Supporting his damaged shoulder with his other hand Lume staggered out unto the tableland. His shredded clothing was blood-soaked from the innumerable cuts caused by splintered wood that had lacerated his unprotected skin like razors. Continuously looking up to the sky he occasionally toppled over before slowly and painfully picking himself up. He heard the distant sonic booms of Ground Support Fighters and Hoppers; sounds he was entirely familiar with. Having scanned the sky through three hundred and sixty degrees, his red and infra-red spectra eyes identified nothing up there.

In the far distance a line of mirror-shiny armour-suited troops appeared over a crag, but Lume did not them, his focus was trained on the sky...

"I have him eyeball, two and a half klicks, 10 o'clock."

"Check. Wait. Brigade this is Grey Viper. We have him, my position. Over."

"Roger Grey Viper. Insulate and contain situation. Friendlies on the way. ETA minutes. Over."

The ground around the advancing troops began erupting haphazardly, slowing them to a trot.

"Roger Brigade, incoming fire, out to you. Hello Facet Black, take Three Section and flank left, draw this off him."

"Roger. Flanking left. Three Section, with me."

The eruptions around the soldiers increased in violence, the ground started to look as if it was boiling. An area in the centre of the effervescing earth became still as a neon blue super extended caterpillar came thundering down into it. The super extended caterpillar changed colour to iridescent mauve as it shrank rapidly in length transforming itself into an alien mound. Then the mound started oozing sixty-metre long caterpillars. Seemingly immune to the surface's seismic activity, the caterpillars zipped off in all directions.

"Holy Shit! One and Two Sections on me, this is our gig. Attack!"

"Grey Viper, this is Voodoo Queen. Mind if we crash your party?"

"Feel free, hit them from the south. Brigade, we need air cover now!"

Some of the troopers advancing at a sprint poured fire into the alien mound as it continued to disgorge caterpillars, shrinking in size as it did - eventually the mound shrank to nothing. Other sections engaged the caterpillars; tracking their rapid jerky stop/start movement with various hand-held weaponry. Most of the fire directed against the mound or caterpillars seemed to be only partially effective. However, when a caterpillar assailed an armour-suited trooper, by whatever mysterious means, he simply exploded from the inside.

"All section, this is Bitter Flame. Grey Viper is down. Press on! Press on!"

As soon as the firing started, Lume had dived for cover by a small rocky outcrop. It wasn't much cover but on the almost featureless tableland it was better than nothing. He now had a ringside view of the battle as it unfolded. Obviously, the armoured infantry was here for him, had tracked his precise location and were attempting to draw the Bulges' fire away from his delicate and unarmoured skin. Equally obvious was the murderously heavy, if somewhat inaccurate, enemy fire that they faced, the greater number of caterpillars and the relative ineffectiveness of the soldiers' weapons.

Then another super extended alien caterpillar thumped down into the middle of this already one-sided battle. From over three hundred metres away, Lume felt the impact of its landing as it jarred his teeth. The super extended caterpillar didn't waste any time in changing colour, shrinking to a mound, and then spewing out caterpillars. Calmly observing the soon-to-be-massacre, Lume was idly speculating that this probably meant the Bulges couldn't transform from wiggling super extended caterpillar directly to regular caterpillar...

He was temporarily blinded by the flash before he was consciously aware of or heard the detonation of whatever it was that had hit the mound. When his vision cleared the mound was still there except it was no longer iridescent mauve just a dull lifeless red colour. Yes, he was sure the mound had unequivocally altered from being alive to being inert. Then his senses, lagging behind actual events, heard multiple sonic booms of Hoppers and Ground Support Fighters. Very accurate and heavy fire started raining down on individual caterpillars.

There were a couple of loud crunches as a pair of mirror-shiny armour-suited feet appeared either side of him. Clearly having jumped a long distance with their suites' strength augmentation and anti-gravity they each reached down, took an arm, and started to pick him up.

"Noooo! Don't stand still. Keep moving!" He tried pushing them away - a futile act against soldiers wearing combat suits.

"*We've got you. Let's go! Let's go!*" They pulled him to his feet even as he struggled.

"You're wired. Keep moving!" Holding him with more than a fraction of the suit's strength would have caused injury. He twisted out of their grasps and dove for the ground as both troopers erupted into ballooning spheres of flying mirror armour, shredded electronics, blood, and guts. Caught in the blasts he was knocked unconscious long before reaching the dirt.

There was a high-pitched shriek as a Hopper, kicking up dust, landed next to the prostrate Lume. Eight mirror-shiny armour-suited troopers jumped out firing; three of them instantly exploded. Two more troopers jumped out, snatched up the bloody battered mess that was Lume and jumped back into the Hopper. Shrieking the Hopper leapt into the air leaving the five standing troopers putting down covering fire. The Hopper was on the ground for less than four seconds.

***

The remnants of the two human fleets, less than a hundred ships, were now meshed into one tight cone formation. The entire raging space battle was in close orbit around Omega Zero Three. As they manoeuvred frantically, both alien and human ships skimmed the upper atmosphere glowing white hot as they did so. Some ships managed to climb back out of the planet's gravity well, while others simply kept plummeting. With the alien ships defragmenting and the human ones disintegrating, the night side sky of Omega Zero Three resembled a colossal meteor shower. Despite the searing incoming fire, the human formation kept its shape and its base towards the planet.

A single tiny Hopper, escorted by several dozen Ground Support Fighters, exited the atmosphere, and flew directly to one of the ships in the cone. Then the entire formation, still unleashing unrelenting fire at the neon blue always changing shape enemy ships, started to move away from Omega Zero

Three. A small formation of about eight ships broke out of the cone and accelerated away from the planet. All the remaining ships in the cone formation went onto the attack to ensure the safe escape of the small flotilla.

***

Three medics in armoured suits, but without helmets, frantically attended to an unconscious Lume, who was lying on a hi-tech stretcher. His camouflage suit was in shreds, an arm was missing at the shoulder, blood gushing, and he was covered with lacerations from the impaled mirror-suit fragments all over his body. Towards the back of the Hopper were a couple of blood splattered fully suited troopers keeping out of the way. As the Hopper settled, there was a gentle tremor and the sound of the engines shutting down.

'*We have docked in Bay 4,*' the Hopper informed them.

"*Lock down! Lock down! Emergency jump in one minute.*"

"We won't have time to get him to MedCen," the first medic complained.

The second medic turned to the team leader. "I don't think he'll survive the jump, Sir."

"Just stop the bleeding and strap him in!" the Captain snapped as he put an oxygen mask over Lume's nose and mouth then added, "Cockpit, this is the extraction medical team, we'll need a Biocontainment shield in Bay 4. Over."

"*This is Flight Command; you'll have Biocontainment ten seconds before jump. Over.*"

"Roger, ten seconds. Out."

As the second medic attempted to staunch the blood flowing from Lume's shoulder, the first started strapping Lume to the stretcher.

"Lock down! Lock down! Emergency jump in thirty seconds."

The first medic finished strapping Lume in and connected him to an intravenous drip. "The nano engines have stopped the bleeding, but he's lost a lot of blood."

"Then let's pray that he hasn't lost too much."

"Lock down! Lock down! Emergency jump in twenty seconds."

The first and second medics hurriedly got into their seats and strapped themselves in. The Captain checked Lume's straps before quickly getting into his seat and strapping himself in then double checking that the troopers had also strapped in.

"If you've ever made a jump outside of a Jump Suite you wouldn't be praying for him, Sir," the second medic added with just a touch of insolence.

"Lock down! Lock down! Emergency jump in ten seconds."

As the Biocontainment shield activated each individual was locked rigidly in place by an invisible force-field. Everything became momentarily fuzzy then flashed sharply back into focus. Next there was a brief but pronounced period of severe juddering as if every single atom in every single molecule was straining to break free. The Hopper's five conscious occupants became instantly befuddled: travelling through hyper-space, even when protected by a biocontainment-field that preserved living tissue, was a harrowing, thoroughly disagreeable experience.

"Biocontainment shielding up! Stand by for one G in five... four... three... two... one! Lock down over. Jump medical teams stand down."

The three medics immediately started vomiting, profusely. As soon as the two troopers finished clumsily taking off their helmets they joined in the puking. The Captain released his seat straps, collapsed to his knees, and crawled, like a drunken dog, over to Lume, retching as he went. The second medic undid his seat straps, attempted to stand, tottered, and collapsed back into this seat. With the suit's strength augmentation, he almost broke the back of the seat.

The Captain wiped spittle from his lips with the back of his gloved hand. "Sit the fuck down or get on your hands and knees, I don't want you staggering around in here wearing that suit."

First and second medics got on their hands and knees and crawled over to help the Captain, who was examining the displays on the stretcher. As all three started working diligently on Lume the third medic said, "There's still severe internal bleeding and his respiration is failing. We need to..."

The Hopper door opened, and a fully armoured suited soldier vaulted in and purposefully bounded over. Unlike the other two troopers, the state of this suit showed that it and its wearer had recently seen some serious combat.

"*Get that mask off, you're poisoning him!*" The suits electronic female voice commanded.

The Captain carefully stood, squared up to the soldier then saw the Gold Stinger badge on the suit. He nodded down to the other medics who took the mask off Lume.

"*What's his condition?*"

"Alive. But he won't be for much longer if you don't get out of the way."

Mary took a pace backwards giving the medics room and the Captain knelt back down. "Change the air mixture to that shit-piece-of-rock we've just left and scan him for germ-line modifications."

The second medic checked a scanner. "No wonder the nano engines took so long, most of his proteins aren't human standard."

"Adjust nanos, stop intravenous drip. Let's see if we can fabricate a more compatible serum."

"There are regeneration and cathartic teams on the way."

"There won't be anything to genetically purge if we don't reverse the treatment we've already administered. I suppose we weren't important enough to be told that he'd been bioprepped."

"Need to know. Just keep him alive, Captain."

Chapter 7

Admiral of the Fleet Akobundu-Tan was standing with her arms folded in the empty corridor by the door to the sickbay of the heavy cruiser *Vale*. Field Martial Hooper, wearing a helmetless battle-beaten-up mirror armoured suit, strode up to her. As he approached, she stared off into space and asked as if thinking aloud, "Is it a Grunt thing?

The Field Martial raised a puzzled eyebrow.

"Or possibly a dick thing?"

Hooper looked back innocently.

"Laurent, I take a very dim view of my Land Forces Commander freelancing." She turned and looked at Hooper." It's *dick*, isn't it?

"On a sacrifice mission such as this it's important for them to know that the boss isn't afraid to get his hands dirty, Ezocaagbo."

"Bullshit! A half a million combat troops going in, but you still couldn't resist playing 'look everybody, see how big my dick is'. And big as you'd like to think it is..." Akobundu-Tan reached across and angrily jabbed at Hooper's badge of rank. "... I gave you those, for your brains.

Hooper gave Akobundu-Tan a wry smile.

Admiral of the Fleet Akobundu-Tan took a half pace up to Hooper and stared coldly up into his eyes. "Pull another stunt like that and I'll not only take them back, I'll have your dick *and* balls as well."

Hooper gave her a suitably penitent look.

"They've only given us a couple of minutes." She turned, manipulated the door controls and the door opened.

This medical centre was ten metre by ten metre, all LCDs and holograms projectors booth. One wall was all glass and beyond the glass was a red lit similar sized room with a heavily bandaged Lume, lying on a bed with lots of cables and tubing attached to him. Katrin and a couple of other senior doctors were sitting, working away at consoles. Mary, back in dress uniform, was standing by the glass looking at Lume. As Akobundu-Tan and Hooper entered the MedCen the doctors made as if to stand, Akobundu-Tan waved them back into their seats. Mary half turned to face Akobundu-Tan and Hooper, still keeping an eye on Lume.

"What's the state of play, Surgeon General?"

"He's taken one hell of a beating but he's stable; drifting in and out of consciousness. However, I don't think he'll be able to talk, Ma'am."

"And why's that?"

"His lungs are shot. The respirators are doing his breathing for him."

Mary paused then turned fully to look at Lume. "I think he's trying to say something."

"Well, let's hear it," the Admiral commanded.

All that issued from the intercom was wheezing and a weak mumbling, then silence.

Katrin checked a monitor. "He's passed out."

"Did anyone catch that?" Hooper asked.

No one responded then Mary said, "I think I made out something like 'prime numbers' but that was all."

"Without seeming insensitive, when are we likely to get some action, Surgeon General?"

"That I can't answer, Admiral. All I can say is that he's on the mend, his chances are fifty fifty."

"Okay, keep us posted." Admiral Akobundu-Tan turned on her heels. "Let's continue our discussion, shall we, Field Martial?" Abruptly she turned back to Mary. "Colonel, sixteen hundred hours, OpsCen, *Pantheon*."

"Ma'am."

***

Admiral Akobundu-Tan and Field Martial Hooper sat in the inner circle of couches and consoles with four Staff Officers sat facing them in the outer circle. They were all busily studying holograms of schematics and text. As Mary entered and approached the Field Officers, the outer circle of chairs and consoles rotated leaving an empty chair facing Akobundu-Tan. Halting in front of the Admiral, Mary saluted and clearly expected to be invited to sit. Akobundu-Tan didn't acknowledge the salute and simply stared back at her for a long moment, leaving her standing rigidly to attention. Eventually the Admiral spoke.

"Are you transsexual?"

"Err, no Ma'am."

"Homosexual?"

"No, Ma'am."

"Bisexual then?"

"No, Ma'am."

Akobundu-Tan turned her attention to the one-way hologram in the air above her. "Your psychological profile makes interesting reading, Colonel. Cutting off a classmate's thumb with a laser scalpel, age nine."

"He pushed me over," all indignant Mary protested.

"Holding down and pouring liquefied pepper into the eyes of a fellow cadet at the Junior Stinger Academy, aged thirteen." Akobundu-Tan paused to examine something in the hologram text in even more detail. "By the age of fifteen you'd really earned the reputation of 'Scary Mary', hadn't you?" Akobundu-Tan looked away from the hologram and locked eyes with Mary. "But, search as I might, I can't find any reference to penis envy."

"Pardon, Ma'am."

Field Martial Hooper averted his gaze, trying desperately not to laugh.

"I want to know where the hell you get off freelancing on one of *my* planetary assaults."

Mary stared back scared, repentant, silent, and standing rigidly to attention.

"When you are ordered to keep your arse space-bound, you keep your arse space-bound. Do you get me loud and clear, Colonel?"

"Ma'am."

Akobundu-Tan shifted in her seat and seemed to relax. "How many Platinum and Gold Stingers have we left in the fleet?"

"Eighteen, Ma'am."

"Actually, it's nineteen." Mary was obviously very surprised by this revelation and the Admiral let that sink in before continuing, "How many norms would commit 800,000 men to recovering just one?"

Mary looked at Hooper who gently shook his head, he wasn't a Stinger. Mary looked back at Admiral Akobundu-Tan with new-found respect and understanding.

"That's right. And I only have eighteen to deploy. So, do as you're damn well told!"

"Yes, Ma'am."

The Admiral sat back. "At ease, sit." She waved Mary into a couch. "Now, six confirmed kills."

"Outstanding! How?" Hooper added his praise.

Mary took a seat but wasn't sure how to react to the compliment. "Double tap, Sir. Something I'd picked up from the Platinum Stinger's reports. He always has his laser set to fire two bursts; the first at one frequency and the second at a higher or lower frequency but same energy output."

Hooper sat bolt upright in his seat. "Anything else?"

Mary looked uncomfortable. "No, Sir."

Hooper turned to Akobundu-Tan. "They and their ships are able to absorb stupendous amounts of energy, without any apparent shielding."

Akobundu-Tan nodded in agreement then looked over to the Staff Officers who all started working away at their consoles. There was silence for several moments as they waited for the Staff Officers.

"There might be something here, Admiral." The Staff Officer seemed hesitant, "We know it takes combined hits from several ships to take them out, but a cursory analysis of their attrition would suggest a cruiser/destroyer combination."

A second, more assured, Staff Officer added, "Our ships have a standard laser configuration. But the destroyers, due to their size, have a different array that fires at a different frequency."

"Let's get a team on this, yesterday." Akobundu-Tan turned back to Hooper. "Over the decades we've worked assiduously at increasing our weapons energy output. Surely it can't be as simple as this."

The Field Martial shrugged. "Solutions to complex problems often turn out to be criminally simple." He tuned to

Mary. "I'll have you on a combat team when this assignment is completed."

Rather than looking pleased Mary gave him an 'it's about time' look. Admiral Akobundu-Tan picked up on this and sat forward. "You're a precious commodity Gold Stinger so let's not go pissing our arse into the wind, shall we?"

"Ma'am."

"Dismissed."

Mary stood, saluted, turned smartly and marched out.

***

Admiral of the Fleet Akobundu-Tan, Field Martial Hooper and a female Staff Officer walked along the corridor towards the Medical Centre of the heavy cruiser *Vale*. Any personnel encountered promptly stepped aside, saluted smartly and then made themselves scarce. Automatically acknowledging the salutes, the Admiral's party continued.

"That's all, 'Is one a prime number?'" Akobundu-Tan asked the Staff Officer.

"That's what he's reported to have said, Ma'am."

"*Is* one a prime number?" Hooper enquired of either.

"Strictly speaking, yes. But, generally, mathematicians tend to ignore it, Laurent."

Hooper pulled a puzzled frown. "Is that significant?"

"Not as far as I can see."

"Nor me, Sir," the Staff Officer concurred.

The group arrived at the Medical Centre and entered. Katrin and the Surgeon General were sitting working. Mary, now dressed in a one-piece Stingers' uniform, was standing looking over Katrin's shoulder at a monitor. Admiral Akobundu-Tan signalled for them to continue.

"He's now conscious, Admiral," the Surgeon General informed them.

"Good. Can we talk to him?"

"Yes, he can hear us."

"Fine." The Admiral looked around and, choosing an unoccupied console, sat and crossed her legs. "In your own time, Platinum Stinger."

Over the intercom came a weak and laboured voice. "*I think their mathematics is based on prime numbers.*"

Everyone took a moment to ponder this then the Admiral sat up and impatiently quipped, "Prime numbers are simply part of the standard real number progression, so a system based on prime numbers is also based on that same progression.

"*I don't think they see it that way, Ma'am. To them non-prime numbers are simply fractions that can be expressed as a computation of prime numbers.*"

"You mean like four being expressed as two plus two?" Hooper asked.

"*Or seven minus three.*"

The Staff Officer took a terminal from her breast pocket and started to tap away on it. Akobundu-Tan became thoughtful. "What led you to this conclusion, Platinum Stinger?"

There was the rasping sound of several ragged deep breaths as Lume gathered the energy simply to speak. "*When I was scouting their base, or whatever it was, I noticed that it was never fixed. It was dissolving and reforming into multiple structures.*"

"Yes, we've witnessed this phenomenon before. So?"

"*I figured that what I was seeing was them continuously constructing, dismantling and reconstructing the structure within minutes.*"

"And?"

"I was trying to calculate the time period of this activity. There weren't any consistent intervals, but I spotted that the number of structures was always a prime number."

"Really? Is that it?" The Admiral sounded doubtful.

"Yes. I know that this seems way off beam, but I think we're dealing with non-static, non-linear entities whose mathematics is based on prime numbers."

The Staff Officer 'Ahemed' an interruption then said, "There might be some mileage in this, Admiral." She leant across to show Akobundu-Tan the terminal. "I've only taken it up to a thousand but there's no number that cannot be express as a computation of up to three prime numbers. So, I guess they'd be able to do all forms of advanced mathematics."

A sceptical Hooper asked, "What's with this non-static, non-linear business, Platinum Stinger?"

Fighting for each breath, it was some considerable time before Lume was able to answer. *"There's no regularity, symmetry, uniformity or rhythm to them or anything they do, Sir."*

The Field Martial pondered for a moment. "I see what you mean, it's almost as if they don't agree that the shortest distance between two points is a straight line."

Katrin looked up from her console and said quietly, "He's slipping."

"We won't get any more out of him today," The Surgeon General confirmed, manipulated some controls on his console and swivelled in his seat to fully face Admiral Akobundu-Tan. "It's been an enduring assumption amongst scientists, particularly the xenobiologists, that mathematics would be a universal language. After all, pi is pi regardless of the species."

"But it isn't if you've never seen a circle..." Hooper said, thinking aloud.

The Surgeon General was equally contemplative. "How can a space-faring species not be conversant with circles?"

"I'm trying to think of anything in nature that's a perfect sphere or circle, and I can't." Mary joined in the conversation.

Katrin looked up from her consoles. "Bubbles are perfect spheres."

"No, they're not," Mary disagreed.

Akobundu-Tan nodded in agreement with Mary before saying, "Non-linear, non-static entities." Pausing as if to digest the concept she nodded to herself then said, "Interesting." Then after staring off into space for a moment the Admiral added, "So we'd be the antithesis of them."

"How so?" Hooper inquired.

Pensively Akobundu-Tan turned to face Hooper. "Regular, symmetric, uniform and systematic."

Katrin excitedly sat up in her seat. "If the Platinum Stinger is even partially right, we might finally be able to communicate with them, Ma'am."

Akobundu-Tan turned to give Katrin a withering look before turning back to Hooper. "Can you think of any of our weapons that are unsynchronized?"

Hooper shook his head. "I'm way ahead of you on this one. Well worth exploring."

The Surgeon General lent over to Katrin and paternally explained, "Matter and anti-matter *cannot* occupy the same space - mutual annihilation."

Akobundu-Tan shot to her feet, she, Hooper, and the Staff Officer spun on their heels heading for the door.

"Carry on."

***

Katrin was alone in the surgical suite of *Vale's* Medical Centre. She sat diligently checking monitors when an instrument to her left beeped and she turned to examine its readouts. She looked through the glass wall at Lume in the red lit treatment room. Still heavily bandage and connected to a web of cables and tubing he seemed asleep. She checked several screens before she was satisfied, then she sat and went back to whatever it was she had been doing.

"*Doctor*," came a barely audible croak over the intercom.

Katrin stood and went into the treatment cubicle. As she approached his bed and stood over him, she saw that Lume's black eyes were weeping. "When was the last time you cried?"

"Is that what's happening to me?"

She busied herself examining readouts. "Sure. Don't you remember ever crying?"

"No."

"Never? Not even as a child?"

"Not that I can remember."

Katrin moved back to him and in her best bed-side manner said, "You've never been conscious during a purge, have you? It's the endocrine system. We need to allow it to get back to its natural balance without medication. Hormones affect the brain; the brain affects the release of hormones; emotional excesses. That's why we usually have the patient on ice while we reverse the bioadaptations. I know it's tough, but you've been kept conscious for debriefs." She moved to examine the attachments around his missing arm. "Look on the bright side and thank the humble worm."

"What?"

"Where are you from?"

"Erbury. You?"

"Panorama. Worms are the insects we emulated in the technique of regrowing limbs."

"I know what worms are, they aerate the soil. We don't have them on Erbury but there are small crustaceans that fulfil the same function."

"Well, thanks to the humble worm from Earth you should have a fully functioning arm within a month or so."

"How long will these emotional excesses last?"

"Unfortunately the endocrine system is the last to stabilise so they'll be with you until we've thoroughly purged the bioadaptations or until the powers that be decide that you've divulged every last detail."

Lume seemed to sink within himself. "So, a few more weeks then."

She nodded, checked a few more bedside readouts, turned, and smiling to herself, went back to the surgical suite and her consoles. She sat and made herself comfortable then had a quick look to check if Lume was looking at her then, with a malicious grin, she started manipulating the controls.

Chapter 8

Admiral Akobundu-Tan and Field Martial Hooper sat facing a couple of Staff Officers. All four were deeply engrossed with the holograms projected above them. A middle-aged woman, clearly a boffin-type but wearing an ill-fitting and untidy army uniform decorated with the rank of a Brigadier entered the OpsCen. She ambled up to them, shuffled to a stop, as opposed to halting, and gave her best shot at a salute but in the end delivered what was more like a distracted wave.

The couches rotated and Hooper nodded her into the empty couch now facing him and the Admiral. "Let's skip the contact report Brigadier, we lost the seven ships taking out five of theirs. What have we learned?"

The Brigadier fidgeted in her seat then began hesitantly, "We've been working with teams on Earth, Rancia, Bacci Five and Cayman. It's clear that we've increased attrition on the enemy but are still just as vulnerable to their weapons. Billions of evolutionary simulations have led to nothing like them. Even our most basic assumptions seem to be lacking some crucial component." She seemed to find being reclined a problem. "This would suggest that there is an unbridgeable chasm between them and us - they seem to be able to utilise randomness, hence their numbering system..."

"So that's bona fide?"

"We think so... Sir. That's the basis of our hypothesis. How can we begin to understand their view of the universe? It is even possible that they do not perceive themselves as being in conflict with us." If she simply lay back, following the contours of the couch, things were so much better. "Clearly they are drawn to order and seem to want to convert it to entropy. We are cascading layers of order..."

"Cascading? What do you mean?" the Admiral enquired.

"As an example: we modified the lasers to variable frequencies. However, the power flowing to the lasers is constant. If we varied that, the generators still run at a steady rate. Even if we varied that as well, the matter/anti-matter reactors have to be kept stable. And that cascade of order applies to all our technology... Ma'am."

Akobundu-Tan pondered for a few moments. "OK, what's the conjecture on the secondary intel re: their ships being made of columns that are composed of the caterpillars, the so-called Bulges, we've encountered?"

The scientist looked uncomfortable. "Well, firstly we have to question whether this intel is actually correct..."

"It's correct," the Admiral interrupted.

The Brigadier looked acutely embarrassed and took a while to respond. "We haven't even a working hypothesis, Ma'am."

"I didn't ask for a working hypothesis."

The scientist squirmed for a while then looked at her feet as if for inspiration before apologetically uttering, "This has caused more controversy and professional clashes than the natural phenomenonist. Even if we accept that all three... forms are different states of the same... entity or entities and that the changes between them are, shall we say, a phase transition similar to the states of matter; solid, liquid, gas and plasma. This still leaves us an enormous problem."

"Which is?" A Staff Officer coaxed.

"While the three different forms may, at least from a rudimentary visual assessment, seem to conserve mass, their movement contradicts the law of the conservation of momentum." The Brigadier gave the impression of having found some inner steel, she straightened and looked the Admiral in the eye. "I know the claims of their sightings have been verified from several source Ma'am, but the laws of physics are fundamental. It ought to be impossible for anything with a mass to come to a complete stop instantly or instantly change direction... and remain intact."

"In the absence of empirical evidence, if you had to make an educated guess..." Hooper enticed.

"I know it's inadequate but if forced to we could only, in good conscience, categorise this capability as 'further unknown technology', Sir," the scientist reluctantly proffered.

Hooper exchanged an exasperated look with Akobundu-Tan before he continued, "So, if we were to take your entropy explanation at face value, what's your best-case scenario?" Hooper asked.

"We see that as leading to a stale-mate, Sir?"

"This is your agreed 'best case'?"

"Yes, Ma'am."

"Thank you, Brigadier."

The Brigadier awkwardly swung her feet off the couch, stood, gave an even less effective salute then turned and ambled out.

"Patch me through to C'n'C," Akobundu-Tan said to no one in particular.

A one-way hologram of the Chief of the Defence Staff, Field Martial Nagy, instantly appeared in front of Akobundu-Tan and Hooper. Field Martial Nagy looked very relaxed and the speed of the connection would suggest he had been expecting Admiral Akobundu-Tan's call. This suspicion was confirmed as he raised an amused eyebrow and asked, "*Is this your pre-emptive strike, Ezocaagbo?*"

Admiral Akobundu-Tan brushed aside this gambit. "Are the Joint Chiefs planning to change strategy to guerrilla warfare, Sir?"

"*That's where we're heading. Now we know their weak spot, we hit and run, keep drawing them away from our solar systems, ensuring losses below the rate of replacement.*" After a long pause he added, "*Plus, who knows what scientific discovery is just around the corner?*"

Admiral Akobundu-Tan now vexed, asserted, "We haven't exactly drawn them away, have we? It's just that they haven't headed into our neck of the woods... Yet!"

Nagy sat back and smiled. "*What's on your mind, Ezocaagbo?*"

"I don't care if we don't understand them and that we never will - *all* lifeforms are averse to pain."

"*You don't think we've found their pain threshold?*"

"No. And when we do, they'll back off. That's the only way to protect our planets."

Admiral Nagy remained affable in contrast to Akobundu-Tan's severity. "*I feel a proposition coming.*"

"Their capacity for pain cannot be infinite. Give me all available ships and I'll take it to them, full-on, around the Omega Zero system."

Admiral Nagy smiled and pondered this for a while. "*Hypothetically, if you had these ships what would you do that's fresh?*"

Admiral Akobundu-Tan sat up, a bloodthirsty look on her face. "In the past even our order of battle has played into their hands. I'd attack without formation and engage without organisation, hunt them down and *annihilate* them."

Nagy gave Akobundu-Tan a 'would you really?' smile, pondered some more then said, *"Let's assume that the Joint Chiefs agree to your highly speculative plan. Let's also assume we martial the vestiges of the third, fifth, ninth and fourteenth fleets* and *their commanders agreed to put themselves under your command, you still couldn't have all available ships."*

"Why not, Sir?"

"We need to keep a sizable presence around each solar system."

"To protect the systems?!" Admiral Akobundu-Tan spat in mock disgust. "That would be like trying to extinguish an inferno by spitting."

"Politically we have to. Also, ships we can easily replace and as they say, 'There's no substitute for experience'. To get this off the ground I'd want sixty percent of your experienced captains and commanders."

"Excuse me Sir, I think there's a fault with the comms. I thought I heard you say sixty percent."

Nagy grinned broadly at Akobundu-Tan. *"Attacking without formation and engaging without organisation does not require experience. In fact, I'd imagine that with inexperience comes a certain unpredictability. It may also be more acceptable, politically, should there be tremendous losses."*

Admiral Akobundu-Tan sank down in her couch seething. "Yes, Sir."

"Let me mull this over and get back to you within twenty-four hours."

"Sir." Akobundu-Tan and Hooper said in unison as Admiral Nagy's hologram faded. Then the Field Martial turned to his immediate superior grinning. "He's as gung-ho as you are. He's also pretty good at arm twisting."

***

What he needed was a mirror. The fleeting reflections he'd glimpsed off the instruments hinted that the corneas of his eyes were now light grey in colour. Had it been his imagination, or had he also spotted a suggestion of delineated irises? He was pretty sure that the lighting was also being subtly adjusted because he thought he was beginning to discern a hint of blueness here and there. Or at least he thought it was blueness. That was the problem with deep bioadaptations - that and the plasticity of the human mind conspiring to make you think you were actually born like this. Who'd ever have imagined that one could forget a colour?

This attempt at using the rate of transformation of his eyes as a proxy to gauge the phase of the purge was simply an act of desperation. The fact that he had the vestige of a new arm growing, was not as heavily bandaged as he had been and was clearly recovering was little solace. Somewhere in the deepest recesses of his mind something was boiling. He'd had hormonal surges before, that was part of the landscape of every bioprep but, this was different, very different. This was like an incessant itch that one couldn't scratch. Over recent days it had grown inexorably in pitch. It would be no exaggeration to say that he was beginning to find it somewhat distressing...

"Can't sleep?" Katrin grinned down at him.

Slightly bemused as to how he could have missed her entering the cubical he shook his head.

She grinned even wider. "That is because of the great-great-grandmother of a hormone surge." Pausing she gave him time to absorb this. "Put that down to me," then she casually asked, "You want to masturbate, don't you?"

He made his face a blank mask and looked back at her.

Leaning forward she deliberately and gently placed both hands around his neck. "When we have patients on ice, we keep their muscles toned. You were far too injured for that," she whispered. "It's quite surprising just how quickly muscles atrophy. You have less than forty percent of your former strength." She tightened her grip. "You're totally powerless and a night hasn't passed where I haven't thought about what you did to me."

He was surprised that she was even bothering to talk - her grasp on his neck said all that needed to be said. Even before entering the Junior Stinger Academy age nine he'd had an innate understanding the subtleties of pain, its anticipation, and its delivery. Then there was the separate matter of not just inflicting pain but causing actual damage to varying degrees of permanency. These multi-facetted nuances he doubted Katrin comprehended... He simply stared back at her.

She released her grip and with a dramatic flourish slipped off her doctors' overalls revealing herself to be naked under them. There was a probability, albeit a vanishingly small probability, that he might possibly have been mildly surprised if she hadn't been naked. Norms were so damn unimaginative and predictable. Getting onto the bed she carefully straddled him while avoiding myriads of tubing and wiring in and around him. She delicately positioned herself on the very tip of his painfully over-engorged member. The deftness with which she accomplished all these manoeuvrings suggested that this was something she'd spent some time planning and rehearsing.

Clamping her hands even more firmly around his neck she checked her balance, checked her vicinity for freedom of movement then ever so slowly and wetly slipped down the shaft of his cock. Leaning down until their noses were almost touching, and with real menace, she whispered, "And pay-back is a bitch!"

***

No, she'd never get completely reacquainted or content with wearing the Stinger uniform - if you could call a one-piece suit with only a solitary inconspicuous Stinger emblem a uniform. Yes, the lack of ornamentation was supposed to signify Stingers permanent, no warning order, battle readiness. She still diligently polished the five anodised buttons and epaulettes bars on her Number One dress uniform on a daily basis. That barely suffice: Stingers' combat boots were made of a camouflaged material that couldn't be buffed and now she was finding it intolerable perambulating in footwear that wasn't mirror shiny. She'd actually, reflexively, got dressed in her Number Two parade uniform when the call had awoken her. She had been nearly out of her cabin before realising her faux pas. Still, for those precious few minutes her garb was comfortable and very comforting.

The Intelligence Chamber was small, cramped and crammed with surveillance equipment. With an unknown and unknowable enemy to fight few resources was being allocated to 'Intelligence'. There was a female Silver and a male Bronze Stinger working furiously away at a battery of consoles.

"What's the flap?"

The Silver Stinger's eyes left the screens for only the briefest moment to acknowledge her presence. "The security sweeps have detected text-comms for the alert parameters you set-up on *Ostal*."

She looked back puzzled.

"The stinger; platinum; relationship; intercourse; liaison; sex; string."

With round the clock appraisal of Lume and the daily trips to *Pantheon* to update the Admiral she wasn't getting much sleep. She waited for the Silver Stinger to elucidate.

"You know, the stuff about a doctor getting it together with one of us."

Mary raised her eyebrows.

"There's been widespread dissemination. We caught all the ones in the fleet, picked up a few on Earth but some got through to Panorama and are probably propagating."

She was now wide awake. "Shit! Panorama military intelligence?"

The Bronze Stinger shifted uncomfortably in his seat before saying, "On the case but the comms was to civilians, so it'll be tricky annulling them without alerting civil authorities."

"That bitch! Copy, expunge and replace all quantum drives that she's had access to. Don't forget to manually sweep *Ostal* as well." Mary spun on her heels, headed out of the Intelligence Chamber, and set off at a full sprint along the deserted corridor.

***

"...and then I'm going to alter your endorphin levels - off the scale and irreversible!" she panted heavily as she bounced up and down on him. "You'll have cravings, craving like an addict's worst nightmare." With her hair soaking with sweat and sticking to her face she peered through its strands like a deranged creature." Wired into my pheromones and mine alone!" Then as if he couldn't work it out for himself while struggling for breath she added, "Zero pleasure fucking any other woman."

Katrin was young and athletic but she was no solider so, as he'd figured, she simply couldn't keep this unrelenting pounding up. She slowly lowered her head, took several long deep breaths, and kissed him forcefully. Then to make the point, she bit his bottom lip and drew blood. "I'll own you, you bastard!

So far, Lume hadn't uttered a single word; his silence consenting to the illusion of her having absolute power over him. So far he, as opposed to his hormones, was amusedly watching this woman work herself into such fervour that she was now on the point of physical exhaustion. So far, he'd recollected five different methods, that he'd become proficient in by the age of fifteen, for killing someone with a single barehanded strike. So far, he hadn't become so engrossed with Katrin and her antics that he'd missed Mary, also out of breath, slithering into the cubical. The storm had nearly run its course...

As Katrin reached a shuddering climax, a laser blast exited her forehead then, in almost comical slow motion, she simply crumpled on top of him. With the all too familiar odour of freshly cauterised human flesh gently wafting around the cubicle Mary strolled over and with some aplomb holstered the laser. Taking in the medical tubing with a single scan as if it were a three-dimensional puzzle, nonchalantly she rolled Katrin off him and the bed like a lump of meat. There was an emphatic 'splat' as Katrin hit on the floor.

It wasn't the done thing to go wandering about spaceships with loaded lasers; so, wherever Mary had come from it was via an armoury and she'd been sanctioned by some seriously high-level authority. He raised a questioning eyebrow.

"She's been blabbing."

Even so he couldn't help feeling that he was owed an apology here. "You could have waited."

"I did, I waited until she came."

"Well I haven't and that's bollocks. You didn't want to hit any equipment."

"You're still hormonal then?"

"Understatement."

She gave him an icy, couldn't-care-less stare. "Don't you have a Sponge?

"You mean that very special, special, not-too-emotionally-stable Norm selected to be my life partner?" No point in trying to hide his sarcasm.

She nodded.

"Strictly between us, Stinger to Stinger?"

Again, she nodded.

"I was hooked-up with a Silver Stinger, Sarah, out of *Islar* before she copped it."

So stunned was Mary by this revelation that she took a couple of tottering steps backwards as if she'd been punched and that provoked Lume, for the first time, to show an emotion approaching anger.

"Yeah, I know!" he spat. "Fight, lay your arse on the line and we'll give you the latitude to do what the hell you like. We might also overlook most of your transgressions. What the heck, we'll even throw in a totally-fucked-up Norm to give you as much pussy or cock as you'd like, because they'll get off on it. But, don't breed!" As suddenly as it had started, his annoyance stopped and, in the blink of an eye, he was back to being his usual stoic self. "Although they'll never admit it, the Norms are shit scared of producing a super-psycho."

He let that hang between them for a while then, in a very reasonable tone, continued, "But there are times when I just wanted some quality sex without the tie me up-humiliate me-hurt me deal - just sex. Who's your Sponge?

"I don't form close relationships."

"Don't or can't?"

"Can't." She turned to leave. "Just as well you've got one good hand then."

"I'd rather you took over where she left off. Minus the squeaky shrieks and the scratches on my neck and chest, mind."

"No."

"Hand jobs I can do for myself. There's a lot to be said for bouncing breasts and the smell of female sweat."

"No."

He took some time looking over Mary's Stinger uniform. "Looks like you've been cleared for ground operations. With the coming engagement, couldn't you do with...?"

She turned back to fully face him. "No."

Slowly sitting up as erectly as he could manage, he stared Mary in the eye. "So, Stinger to Stinger, you saying that you didn't feel the slightest *tingle* when you freelanced?"

She shrugged noncommittally then became resolute. "We *are* super-psychos. It's a hyper-psycho that the Norms worry about."

Nodding in agreement he smiled. "So, coming up behind someone and excavating their brains didn't get any juices going?"

"Lume, the Norms are right."

"Evasion! So, it did get you just a tad moist. And she's dead because there's no outlet for all that 'tension'." He paused for a moment. "This isn't about relationships or fatherhood - just good old fashion, straight up, sex."

After staring at him blankly for a very long while, she abruptly turned and strode out of the cubicle. Just as abruptly she halted, spun on her heels, and marched back up to his bed. There was another interminable long pause before she took a deep breath and frigidly started to undress. As she did this, he leant over to look down at Katrin on the floor.

"A Stinger clean-up squad will be along later." She passed in her undressing and gave him a cold stare. "Laugh and you're dead. But... I've never... I'm... I'm a virgin."

Lume stared back, dead pan. "I'm not laughing, Gold Stinger."

Chapter 9

Every one of the hundred odd couch/consoles in the OpsCen was reclined and manned by personnel dressed in battle armour. All the command staff had their combat helmets off but next to them ready to be donned at a moment's notice. Holograms of ship deployments, various schematics of the Omega Zero system and myriad other data danced, filling the air over the central circle of couches. Above the low background hum of innumerable, anxious conversations was the hypnotic rhythm of hundreds of armoured-gloved fingers tapping away at touch-sensitive controls. In contrast to the hive of activity around her, Admiral Akobundu-Tan, with a hyped-up Field Martial Hooper sitting next to her, took an unhurried dispassionate assessment of the OpsCen.

It had taken individual face-to-face meetings with each of the four flag officers she now commanded. Without a field promotion each was the same rank as her; each with a distinctive modus operandi and pretty firm views on how 'it ought to be done'. Admiral of the Fleet Susanna Choi-Tan, the illustrious commander of the ninth fleet, had been particularly problematic and not just purely on professional grounds: in their private relationship, truncated as it was, Ezocaagbo accepted that Susanna had appropriated the 'big sister' role for herself. Even so, by picking them off individually she had brought to bear maximum leverage along the persuasion/coercion spectrum in getting her way. She suspected that Nagy had kept the field promotion in his back pocket just to see if she would hack it. Such were the politics of commanding, but in the end this operation would be executed according to her wishes.

Eventually, almost languidly, she said, "Patch me through to all stations." A Staff Officer promptly nodded to her.

"This is Admiral Akobundu-Tan. For twenty-seven years we've been given a comprehensive and one-side walloping by the enemy. For twenty-seven years we've taken it. Today that stops. Today is the day of retribution! You have your orders. Jump when ready. Kill anything that moves!" She signalled the Staff Officer to cut comms.

"Lock down! Lock down! Combat jump in twenty seconds!"

Everyone in the OpsCen calmly, and without interrupting whatever activity they were engaged in, donned their combat helmets. Each couch then auto-strapped its occupant in as the lighting in the OpsCen dimmed.

"Lock down! Lock down! Combat jump in ten seconds!"

The biocontainment shield snapped on, pinning them even more firmly to their couches as the artificial gravity just as abruptly terminated. As always, everything became bleary for a while before refocusing. As always, there were the severe teeth-chattering vibrations through everyone and everything. Then there was the inevitable puking up in combat helmets which had been designed with that eventuality in mind.

"Biocontaiment shielding up! Stand by for one G in five... four... three... two... one! Lock down over! Weapons free!"

Akobundu-Tan and Hooper, who had been making super-light jumps before most of the OpsCen personnel were born, focused in on and were already assessing projections, before the artificial gravity returned. The Field Martial pointed up to something but before he could speak the Admiral nodded -

they had fought so many battles together - and touched a button on her console.

"Susanna, I know it goes against the grain but disperse your formation. If you hunt as a pack, you'll draw them to you. Give your Captains their head."

A one-way head and shoulders hologram of a similarly armour suited Eurasian woman appeared before them; only they could see it or hear any dialogue. *"We've got mutual fire support, Ezocaagbo."*

"Just do it, Admiral!"

Admiral Choi-Tan gave a prompt nod and her hologram vanished.

"It's the Captain," a Staff Officer informed them.

Akobundu-Tan nodded assent and another one-way head and shoulders hologram appeared; this time of a man of African descent, in the midst of removing his combat helmet, and seemingly far too young to be a Captain.

"Sorry to interrupt Ma'am, but I'm having difficulty shedding the frigates and destroyers," the Captain informed her from *Pantheon's* command centre which was also an independent Jump Suite that was several hundred metres distant.

Of course, this was more than a habit, it had been drilled into every one of them since they were Cadet Midshipmen at the Naval Academy; protect the Flag Ship at all cost. By simply making eye contact with the Captain's hologram she acknowledged his statement and it disappeared. Then with the merest raising of a finger her orders were transmitted to their escorts, as was briefed, to abandon defensive duties and become free-ranging hunters. She slowly turned to Hooper, a stern look on her face.

"For God's sake Laurent, stop fidgeting!" After a suitably long pause she smiled then added, "Now just piss off and go do your big dick thing."

Field Martial Hooper, Commander of Land Forces, bounced out of his seat and, like an overeager schoolboy, dashed out of the OpsCen. A Staff Officer slipped into the vacated couch next to the Admiral.

*****

Thirty-five fully mirror-suited and armed troopers sat strapped into their acceleration couches, in two rows facing each other on either side of the Hopper. No puking or wooziness here; these were already suited & booted assault marines who, along with their entire drop division, had made it from the various Jump Suites to the Hopper bays at the double as soon gravity had been restored. This particular bay on *Vale* held sixty-one similarly laden Hoppers and the heavy cruiser had over twelve such autonomous launch bays.

Also suited but with her helmet in her hand, Mary coolly strolled down the aisle between the troopers. With their helmets on she couldn't have seen their faces let alone look into their eyes, but she deliberately paused and turned to look at each visor as if she could. Even when seated nearly all the troopers were taller than her but the distinct Stinger's solo-killing-machine armoured suit said all that needed to be said about its wearer. Reaching the end of the line, she turned and paused to look over the assembled then bellowed, "This is for the human race. Hit the ground firing. Ram and scram! You heard the Admiral, kill everything that moves!"

Roaring, all the marines punched the air, then Mary jumped into her couch, strapped in and clamped her helmet on - it was now a matter of seconds before they launched.

***

The half-moon crescent of the planet Omega Zero Three filled the sky like a spectacular ruby hanging in space. All was serene then... the momentary eye-watering flares as human ships, in ones and twos, started to materialise from hyper-space into low orbit. On re-entering normal spacetime each ship commenced unleashing unremitting fire - lasers, railguns, and missiles - down into the atmosphere while simultaneously launching Ground Support Fighters and Hoppers. The instant each craft was launched it immediately executed a series of random high-G turns before diving towards the planet.

More and more human ships continued to arrive, each taking its own orbit and flying its own course. By the time the first of the enormous neon blue, always changing shape, enemy ships appeared there was a sizable but confusing mishmash of human ships gathered around the planet. This time the enemy ships materialised into a blizzard of depleted uranium, laser, and missile fire. Taking multiple hits, they spontaneously started fragmenting into the wiggling like columns. As the surviving rope-like columns tried to recombine they were hit again and again and kept under a systematic pounding.

By the second, scores of alien and human ships continued to appear. Without a moment's pause or hesitation, they instantaneously set about inflicting devastation on each other. The noticeable difference between the opposing forces was that the human ships were disgorging Hoppers and Ground Support Fighters like gigantic beasts haemorrhaging globules of flaming black and silver blood.

Despite having the whole Omega Zero system available as a combat zone, Admiral Akobundu-Tan, by deploying and concentrating her forces around a single planet, had by any standards of space warfare, drawn the enemy into a claustrophobic close-quarter-battle with overlapping murderously accurate and destructive fire. More importantly, for the first time in twenty-seven years of continuous, if somewhat dispersed conflict, the humans were inflicting significant attrition on the enemy.

The overlapping murderously accurate and destructive fire wasn't all one-way, but this knife fight in a phone booth space battle, was throwing up some new and disturbing insights on the 'unknowable' enemy. Each enemy ship entered the fray normal size, roughly six to seven times the mass of the largest human dreadnought. Yet, if the now very effective human fire systematically whittled one down to, say, a quarter its original mass it still seemed able to preserve its original destructive capability. More alarmingly it was now painfully clear that if even two of the wiggling rope-like columns, any two from any alien ship, interlaced this constituted a new 'ship' - a ship that remained fearsomely effective at demolishing the human opposition.

There had been little enough room for manoeuvring to begin with, but even more alien and human ships swarmed into the planet hugging, low orbit. Engagements were at such short ranges that missiles were armed as they were launched and whatever it was that the aliens' weapons did, they seemed able to do it much more effectively at close range. The congestion had now built until manoeuvring was nigh impossible leading to the real danger of ships colliding with friendlies, hostiles, or wreckage.

***

The battle above Omega Zero Three was rapidly transforming its thermosphere into a spherical crust saturated with two-metre-thick, kilometres long, dull red columns and breached, atmosphere spewing, disintegrating human ships. On the night side of the planet another spectacular meteor shower embroidered the sky courtesy of the debris caught by the planet's gravitational field; this time the immense artificial light show was embellished with intense pulsating planet-bound weapon fire.

On the day side, from one distant boundary of the horizon to the other, tens of thousands of the wiggling alien columns could be seen rising up, through intense laser and missile fire raining down from above. Some took multiple hits and plummeted back to the ground. Others made it to high atmosphere then interlaced to form the neon blue enemy ships that then winked out of existence.

At fifteen thousand metres, a Hopper, executing high-G evasive manoeuvres, winged through the cloud of rising columns. Flying straight and level for a couple of seconds it ejected four troopers then went back to high-G manoeuvres. Continuing its erratic course for several more seconds it then stabilised to eject four more troopers. Just as it resumed its evasive manoeuvres the Hopper exploded violently from the inside becoming just another flaming streak across the sky.

The last trooper to exit was caught in the blast and blown backwards and upwards into a retrograde parabolic arc. The ragdoll of a mirror-suited figure created its own shockwave as it tumbled wildly through the sky. Though designed to absorb blasts and sudden impacts the abrupt acceleration of the explosion inevitably rendered the suit's occupant unconscious. When the trooper eventually ceased streaking upwards to start their long descent the violent rotation began to ease off, however, in the thin upper atmosphere, the velocity of their plunge rapidly increased to supersonic speeds.

The isolated individual plummeted like a stone to a height of about fifteen hundred metres before the suited trooper seemed to regain a semblance of consciousness. It took a few more moments before the imperilled individual became cognisant of their immediate situation and started to flay wildly, grasping at air. Perceiving non-intelligent control, the suit's automatics activated the anti-gravity at three hundred and fifty metres from impact. Derived from the rate of descent this height was calculated by the automatics to minimise exposure to enemy fire yet given sufficient time to slow without the deceleration itself causing further harm to the supposedly injured occupant.

The combat suit touched down on its left side with a weight of less than a gram. Over the next twelve seconds, while the automatics assured themselves that it was resting on something solid, the artificial gravity reduced to zero - the point eight G weight for Omega Zero Three. It initiated a self-check - being an electromechanical process this took less than half a second: all systems fully operational; power levels ninety-eight percent. As it instructed the primary and secondary bio-systems to initiate the much longer process of assessing the damage to its organic occupant, the occupant overrode this with a command to roll to its right and get to its feet.

She drew the laser from her back simultaneously with springing nimbly to her feet. A three sixty scan revealed that the nearest of her platoon was some thirty odd kilometres away. The Hopper had been destroyed, bits still falling and something fairly large was about one and a half klicks away, rapidly zig-zagging its way in her general direction.

She couldn't have written the script any better. Yes, she was a Colonel in the regular marines and had even commanded an assault regiment. All because someone back at the Stinger academy had opined that she demonstrated strong leadership aptitude. This she'd thought odd at the time because she was an incorrigible misanthrope. She could just about tolerate being in moderately close proximity to other people: which presented unique challenges in the confines of a combat spaceship. Truth be told it was the dress uniforms, especially the warm weather Service Dress uniform, that kept her assuaged in the role as a regular marine.

Then someone, an individual who she'd assumed was clearly mentally deficient, saw fit to transfer her from her frontline elite troops and combat duties to Stinger Ops. At the time if she could have identified and then got to that individual, she'd slaughtered them on sight. Now, she had a pretty shrewd idea of just who that individual was and accepted that there were bigger pictures which she could only guess at. Now, at last, she was back where she belonged - in combat. Now, she had another assault regiment to command. Now, her drop platoon was kilometres distant and who knew where the rest of the regiment was dispersed. They hadn't even registered on the scan.

Nobody to command or nursemaid was just fine; first and foremost, she was a Stinger - a Gold Stinger. Stingers were first and foremost, autonomous creatures. With an emotion approaching elation she did some rough and ready calculations on the image projected onto her visor before firing two mortar rounds from her back launcher. Then she sprinted off to her left; some instinct telling her that, assuming the mortars were ineffective, this was the direction the fast approaching enemy would be zigzagging in from.

Less than three hundred metres away, a tall alien column changing colour to neon blue and started its erratic climb. If it hadn't been for Lume's debriefs on this particular capability of the enemy she'd have doubted her vision. Why hadn't it shown up on her scan? It had been static and these things, as far as she knew, didn't broadcast on any EM frequency that's why. With a burst of speed, she started her own zigzagging, moving in on the column while pouring fire into it. All lasers, from the ship borne monsters to handheld side arm, had now been reconfigured to fire multi-frequency pulses.

As she closed the distance to the column she, along with gravel, foliage, and anything moveable within a couple of hundred metres, was caught in its anti-gravity field. Deciding that she'd done enough tumbling for one day, she overrode the suit automatics which were no doubt concluding that it ought not to be ascending thus a negative ant-gravity field needed to be generated. Rising amidst the cloud of debris she reclined into the horizontal and, keeping the rifle butt pressed firmly into her shoulder, continued to hammer accurate fire into the column. She was fairly certain that this fire was having some effect because this column didn't appear to be rising as rapidly as others.

Just as she'd loaded the third laser energy pack, she and her accompanying haze of landscape stopped rising and hung there for a moment. The readout said she was one thousand, two hundred and sixty-seven metres above ground. Abruptly the wiggling column accelerated skywards, and Mary started to plunge. By way of a goodbye she cut loose with another two mortar rounds from her back launcher - not directly at the column but at where she estimated it was going to be. Only then did she release her override to instruct the suit's automatics to do their thing.

With genuine surprise, she saw the detonation of both mortar shells in close proximity to the receding column. It was an even greater surprise to observe the column curtailing its rapid ascent; it seemed to hesitate for a second then started to lose height - not exactly falling, more a sedately fluttering down. Interesting! She was falling much faster than the alien column but, in horizontal separation terms, was still less than a couple of hundred metres from it. With pure combat instincts, rather than computation, she instantly scripted the coming ground battle and its likely outcome ... she was falling faster but not fast enough.

Mary again overrode the automatics and called for maximum negative ant-gravity while executing aerial gymnastics as she did. She hadn't forgotten about that other zig-zagging contact either; she needed to land running and firing. There was a gut-wrenching moment as the suit abruptly started hurtling down; she didn't let that faze her, leaving the deceleration details to the automatics, she went back to simulating the one-on-two battle in her head.

Satisfied, she started scanning the rapidly approaching landscape beneath her. Just as the suit began to decelerate at an altitude of about four hundred and fifty metres, she spotted the Bulge. It had been moving away from the general area in a series of haphazard surges then in one spurt, and with an awesome turn of speed, it was back, less than eight hundred metres from where she and its big brother would likely be touching down.

She didn't consciously instruct the suit to instantaneously bounce up and to the left. She only became consciously aware of it when her body registered, after-the-fact, the painful seventeen Gs' of momentary lateral acceleration. All she was conscious of was the vague thoughts that if she had a fix on the Bulge, it probably had a fix on her and that falling in a ballistically calculable straight line was probably unwise to say the least.

Once her eyeballs decided to settle back into their respective sockets they decided, of their own accord, to focus on roughly where she would have been had the suit not executed its seventeen Gs' shimmy. Then they had the impudence to try sending messages to her brain that they were witnessing airburst explosions. Her brains knew that what the eyes were seeing was nothing like any explosions they'd ever seen before therefore it struggled to formulate its own interpretation of the 'data'. The air approximately where she would have been was - the best depiction her brain could concoct of the information from her eyes - 'effervescing.' As if, suddenly, mid-air, there was a cascade of simultaneous implosions and explosions of invisible balloons.

Then she was down! The instant her feet touched terra firma, she bid bon voyage to the final brace of mortar rounds setting them on an expedition towards the still indirectly approaching Bulge. Without a moment's pause to admire her handiwork, she set off at the maximum thirty-four kilometres per hour sprint of the suit, heading away from the where she concluded the column would touch down. Still on the move she detached and ditched the now surplus-to-requirements mortar launchers in time to hear the dull concussion of her motor rounds landing. The Head-up Display (HUD) told her 'close enough.'

This positive bulletin was immediately neutralised by a third concussive reverberation and she didn't need the HUD to enlighten her that this was the result of the column thumping down. Abruptly changing direction to move tangentially but always in the general direction of the column she squeezed out a few more k.p.h. from the suit. It was a simple plan really: keep the column between her and the Bulge. She didn't know for a fact but all the intelligence they had, suggested that the enemy was fairly inert when in column mode; seemingly only able to inflict their mystifying damage in the Bulge or interlaced ship form.

She'd discharged one complete energy pack of sustained laser fire into the column and had reloaded a second pack before it changed colour from neon blue to mauve and began to shrink in size. Then in a dawdling sort of fashion, the still contracting column took its time budding and then shedding one Bulge. In fact the Bulge took so long to emerge that by the time it was completely detached it had been doused with so much of the second energy pack's fire that it simply ground to a standstill and turned a dreary red colour.

Using both the suit's mechanics and anti-gravity, Mary jumped a hundred metres to her left. When she landed her peripheral vision hinted that something extremely unpleasant had occurred in the general area of where she had been standing. Letting off a couple of bursts at the column she jumped again, this time following the laser pulses directly towards the column and landing only about ten metres from it. The still slowly transforming column was making a bad job of squeezing out another Bulge. It was definitely damaged, incapacitated, dysfunctional and generally off its game. Double tap, one burst into the pupating Bulge and one into the column itself then she jumped again.

Time for the main event.

The iridescent mauve streak came into view roughly where she'd anticipated it would appear, but it was moving considerably faster than she expected. So fast that she couldn't get a shot off. Simultaneous with her instructions for the suit to jump was the entire area around her erupting in a cacophony of concussive multiple booms and flying earth and gravel. Landing and immediately jumping again she concluded that she'd escaped the barrage unscathed but, unfortunately and much to her chagrin, her mirror shiny combat suit wasn't mirror shiny anymore.

She landed with her laser rifle tucked into her shoulder and sighted along it but, of course, the Bulge was no longer there. Where? Tracking left then right her HUD locked on the target and she swung around further to her right.... Four, fifty metres, in her sights, she fired - double tap - and the stopwatch in her head said, 'Time to go'. The blast that knocked her off her feet said, 'Too slow'. With several suite diagnostic warnings flashing on the HUD she guessed that counted as a near miss. No need to get overly excited by the HUD warnings, if it had been a hit she'd have literally been in bits.

Flipping back up onto her feet, full sprint, abrupt change of direction, jump. Now, she was decidedly and venomously aggravated: her custom-made, immaculately reflective Stinger's armoured suit had been overlaid in a coating of grimy ochre filth. She reacquired the target, which was now at a range of one, seven, eight metres and hit it with six rapid but spitefully accurate pulses. Her brain was just getting around to instructing the rest of her body and its symbiotic armoured suit to 'move' as she saw the Bulge transform from a life affirming shimmering mauve to a dearly departed dismal red.

'Got yah...!'

Without any warning, she was in the middle of a magnitude 9 on the Richter scale earthquake with only the suit's gyroscopes keeping her upright. Belatedly the HUD informed her that there were now three more Bulges in the vicinity. That the HUD target tracker hadn't given her prior notice meant that they'd simply 'arrived'. Where was the only place they could have arrived from? As she kicked in the anti-gravity to spring out of the earthquake zone, she looked around at the column, which was no longer so much a column, it was only a ten-metre high blob.

Another mystery: if the column was poorly how come its budded Bulges appeared to be disgustingly healthy and fighting fit? And there was no way she could survive a one-on-three. She didn't dwell overly long on her non-prospects: kill the column before it spawned any more Bulges and before the new players killed her! There, a simple, achievable, and closing objective.

Feeling almost contented she turned and with a burst of speed headed back indirectly towards the column. Now, wherever she moved to, the ground around her started to erupt after a couple of seconds on a particular trajectory. Despite always moving unpredictably and getting off about half a dozen bursts into the column she was gradually being bracketed by the increasingly accurate enemy fire.

Why were her molars hurting her? Her jaw was clamped ferociously tight, that's why? On the remote off chance that it actually exited, she guessed that it wasn't the done thing to enter the afterlife petulant, cussing and right royally pissed off. And that's exactly what she'd do if she were blown to bits by that column's three Bulges before she got the satisfaction of killing it.

Loading her penultimate energy pack, she summoned the antigravity and jumped to land less than five metres from the blob. It had been her intention to stand with solemn fortitude, rooted heroically and majestically to the spot, until she had discharged at least half of the energy pack. Although there had never been any speculation on the matter, clearly the enemy was on familiar terms with the concept of friendly fire because as all hell broke loose around her, less than five metres away, the blob was insufferably unaffected by any of it.

As gravel ricocheted off every surface the raucous din inside the combat suit was like being inside an empty can pelted with a million pebbles. Yes, she had a stubborn streak, but discretion was the better part of valour, plus staying put was inimical to her general wellbeing. Try something different. She jumped thirty metres or so, landed and immediately bounced back to the exact spot she'd vacated.

A brief wait but she learned that it took them nearly as long to reacquire her; long enough for her to completely empty the energy pack into the blob with one uninterrupted burst and note its deeply satisfying transition from mauve to dull red. Using anti-gravity and mechanics she launched herself into a backwards somersault like a low-level missile. Putting distance between herself and the Bulges she had the last energy pack loaded by the time she touched down. To say one energy pack against three Bulges was inadequate would be the understatement of understatements - this was for just for pride and being a general nuisance.

As the HUD showed the Bulges rapidly zipping their circumlocutory way towards her it also chose, rather unkindly she thought, that moment to inform her that power levels were now only eight percent. Perhaps she ought not to scold the suit so severely, it had been trying to draw her attention to the rapidly diminishing power situation which she had chosen to ignore. Pity she wouldn't get a chance to report the good tidings on the bounce back phenomena...

First, she perceived in the visible spectrum, the effect of the cascade of missile fire from above - the eye-watering, white-heat, ballooning stadium-sized fireballs in three distinct locations. Then, she heard the sharp, teeth-grating hypersonic crack conjoining seamlessly into the high-pitched banshee screech of the actual rocket motors. Next, she was buffeted by the searing blast waves from the explosions and the suit, perhaps in an act of penance, had the good manners to inform her that there had been a spike in the ambient temperature but it was nothing she need fuss over. Finally, she heard the sonic boom of a Ground Support Fighter whizzing past somewhere overhead.

More often than not she was extremely sensitive to loud noises but on this occasion, she thought she would just go with the flow.

"Scary Mary, this is Blue Five Zero. Stand by for extraction and reinsertion to your unit. Hopper inbound, ETA two minutes."

"Roger Blue Five Zero. Naked. Over."

"Copy that, naked. Will remain on station. Out."

Not being one prone to outbreaks of unwarranted optimism she only allowed herself a smallish sense of gladness at having her personal Ground Support Shepherd. The gladness then took it upon itself to implement a minor fillip when she heard the distinct whine of a steadily approaching Hopper. Simultaneous with the delinquent fillip of gladness the HUD had the impudence to advise that the Ground Support Fighter was no longer there - and it wasn't one of those no longer theres as in having departed. Taking a fleeting look up to a height of about five thousand metres she saw that where her airborne minder ought to have been there was now a stunning multi-coloured cascade of flaming confetti.

Then, just to round things off, the soles of her boots outdid the HUD in informing her that another alien column had just touchdown in the close vicinity. Asserting its pre-eminence, the HUD flaunted its superior capabilities by imparting direction and a distance to target of less than three hundred metres. Oh well, it wasn't blindingly obvious to her how the Hopper would be able to extract her before the newly arrived column sprouted several more Bulges. Damn, this is typical of the deep poo that fillips of gladness tend to land you in...

"Scary Mary, this is this Blue, Five, Five. Sit tight!"

In the fractions of a second it was taking her to compose a suitable pithy riposte; something along the lines of, 'Easy for you to say, you aren't about to be up to you armpits in Bulges.

Now fuck off and die, Atmosphere-jockey,' a sustained volley of hypersonic missiles eradicated the column and its immediate environs of anything reminiscent of life. Being well within the blast zone the sequential and disturbingly psychedelic shockwaves from the multiple detonations simply lifted her off her feet and tossed her around like a feather in a whirlwind. With the automatics working overtime she was able to land on her feet as the maelstrom eased off. All things considered, perhaps she ought to stay her intended haranguing of the Atmosphere-jockey.

Firmly shutting the fillip of gladness in a suitable emotion-proof receptacle she placed the laser on her back and adopted a feet apart star stance. The Hopper came into view flying at a height of fifty metres, travelling at a regulation two hundred k.p.h. As it flew over her, its tractor beam jerked her off the ground and she started a rapid but steady ascent. About ten metres from the Hopper she was suddenly sucked into the back of the transport. It wasn't at all surprising to see that it was already occupied by several other soldiers who had also obviously been having their fill of fun too. She was about to 'Take Command' by demanding a SitRep...

"Strap in! Stand by for high-G manoeuvres!" the Hopper ordered.

The craft remained straight and level for the few seconds it took her to comply then it stood on its tail and rocketed straight up in a vertical supersonic climb.

***

The dancing holograms illuminated the air displaying the utter chaos surrounding Omega Zero Three. Amongst the drifting debris of human ships and rigid dull red alien columns, the far-flung battle was raging between thousands of alien and human ships. There was no pattern or order to the battle just a confusing mass of ships manoeuvring bewilderingly; blazing laser fire; missile salvos; ships exploding or fragmenting into wiggling columns. It was impossible to discern which side was inflicting the greater attrition.

This pictorial representation of the external carnage was in marked contrast to the utter calm of the low-voiced orders being issued and replies received in the OpsCen. All personnel still had their helmets on and were strapped firmly to their couches. They had been engaged in this brutal space-born mêlée for several hours now yet all the OpsCen personnel appeared to be in an almost Zen-like state of calmness. You didn't progress to ops on the bridge of even the smallest ship, let alone the very nerve centre of a fleet, if you hadn't unswervingly demonstrated a serious 'keep your head whilst all those around you are losing theirs' aptitude.

Admiral Akobundu-Tan calmly looked up at the holograms then touched a panel by the side of her couch. "Captain, if I were to take my eyes off the big picture for a moment, I'd note that we've only had two kills. Now run it down and stomp on it!"

A hologram of the Captain materialised. *"On it, Ma'am."* Then it disappeared.

Then, the Operations Centre shuddered, lights and holograms flickered, power indicators quivered, air pressure decreased then stabilised. Distant alarms started wailing, signifying that forced fields had been breached and sections of the enormous ship had been holed and was venting atmosphere - *Pantheon* had taken a significant hit.

"I said, stomp on it, not, toy with it, Captain."

"We're coming around for another pass, Ma'am." This time the Captain had the good sense not to expose himself to her withering stare.

The Admiral turned to one of her Staff Officers. "What's the situation planetside?

"Difficult to say, Ma'am. I think we're holding our own."

She drummed her fingers on the side of her couch for a few beats...

"Call up the reserves. Commit all ships. Let's really take it to them."

***

The maze of cables and tubing surrounding Lume had steadily reduced in density recently. This he'd taken to be an inverse indicator of his rate of recovery. Fortunately, the dwindling plumbing had also cleared a small space above his bed. Now propped up gingerly on pillows, he could comfortably view the images projected into this space; images of the ultrahigh attrition space battle around Omega Zero Three. The hologram had been tuned to his still adjusting eyes and he was told that someone with normal eyesight would have seen only vaguely blurry shapes. That this reprogramming was done at all hinted, most surprisingly, that his wishes carried some weight on the heavy cruiser *Vale*.

***

The night sky, from horizon to horizon, was illuminated by the continuous flaring of massive detonations high in the atmosphere. Beyond the atmosphere, hundreds of pinpricks of starlight streaked erratically across the sky; many abruptly flashed momentarily then streaked comet-like, gradually winking out of existence. The stroboscopic flashes and what appeared to be successive gargantuan meteor showers accompanied by thunderous reverberations added to the impression of a planet-wide fireworks celebration.

On the ground a soldier was running, dodging side to side towards an alien mound in the near distance. As he closed on the mound, a Bulge zipped in from the left and the area around the soldier erupted, tossing him into the air. The Bulge then zipped up to and merged with the mound. The soldier landed on his feet and kept up his side to side charge, pouring fire into the mound. Many dozens more Bulges, all taking intense ground laser fire from several directions, darted up to and start fusing with the alien mound. It began to lengthen and change shape to a wiggling column. The wiggling column started to rise...

"Jump! Jump! Don't let it bolt."

Still firing, Hooper kicked in the anti-gravity and vaulted high into the air towards the rising column. Against the intermittent total blackness of the night were several other parabolic arcs of laser fire hitting the column. Hooper landed, bounced high again and continued to fire. Even more of the soldiers seemed to have cottoned on to his idea of using antigravity to get higher than the column to fire down at it. Even so much of this laser fire ended in the abrupt mid-air flash of an exploding armoured suit; meaning that there were still plenty of Bulges still on the ground.

At about a hundred metres the column gradually stopped rising, hung there for a brief moment then crashed to the ground and in the planet's weak gravity toppled over in slow motion.

He checked his HUD; there was another mound and over thirty of those nasty alien caterpillars in the vicinity. *"There's another one, one and a half kilometres to the north. Watch out for Bulges. Move in! Keep in on the ground!"*

The combination of night vision and the HUD icon readout confirmed what he'd begun to suspect. All the Bulges, with their irregular zippy movements, were heading for the mound and fusing with it and the mound was changing to a wiggling column. For the first time ever, they had the enemy on the run.

***

Admiral Akobundu-Tan folded her arms while looking up intently at the holograms. What these images and symbols depicted, on a solar system-wide scale, was that, in terms of attrition, the battle had passed the tipping point. If she kept the initiative and momentum, over the next hour or so, despite taking more heavy losses she would systematically grind down the enemy. Whatever the aliens' rationale for trying to secure Omega Zero Three it would have come to nought. That much was clear, what she was pondering, without hitting on an obvious solution, was how to minimise further losses.

A Staff Officer turned to her. "Admiral, they're withdrawing from the planet!"

She nodded to the Officer, drummed her fingers on the side of the couch and focussed on the image of the planet and the holographic information accompanying it. All indicators suggested that this was indeed a full-scale planetary withdrawal. Keeping up the pressure, her land forces were hammering away at the retreating enemy and extracting a heavy toll. However, mid atmosphere was where they were most vulnerable, so her ships and atmospheric fighters were having a field day chopping those long wiggling columns to pieces.

Had it been her that was withdrawing she would have used her ships in orbit to cover the lift from planet. But true to form of never doing anything that made a blind bit of sense the enemy ships in orbit carried on with the tumultuous action as before. She drummed her fingers even more; this was becoming too easy...

"It's the Platinum Stinger from the *Vale,* Ma'am. He insists," another Staff Officer informed her.

She raised a finger and a head and shoulders hologram of Lume, much recovered since she last saw him, appeared before her. "Platinum Stinger or not, I'll have you tossed into space for interrupting me mid-engagement. So, let's hear it. And it had better be good.

"This doesn't smell right, Ma'am."

"You're a spectator not a participant!"

"It's getting hot so they're leaving the kitchen." He paused for a moment. *"That's too logical, too comprehensible, too..."*

"Too human?" Something about this had begun to bother her too. She drummed her fingers for a few more beats. "Lift our people out of there, now!

It was a marvel to behold; her mere words put instantly into such dynamic action. The holographic icons showed thousands of Hoppers immediately switching from infantry mobility, resupply and Casivac to drop retrieval. And although their instruments weren't that accurate at registering the enemy unless they were actually moving, she was pretty sure she'd have all her forces off planet before they did. This was a drill they had down pat - they could lift and retreat in minutes. After all, how many times had she been forced to hitch up her skirt and run away after being right royally butt-fucked by them?

"All ships join the low orbit party. Thermosphere retrieval and stop their columns making it to orbit."

Raining down lasers and missiles on the rising columns was all well and good but... A lump of depleted uranium accelerated to a respectable fraction of light speed fired into a planetary atmosphere? All the kinetic energy would dissipate as millions of degrees heat and an enormous shockwave, wouldn't it? The projectile would simply evaporate.

"Bring the railguns into play."

"I'd say that I'm pretty inventive Admiral, but I'd never think of using a railgun as an area weapon." Lume was staring at her with a mixture of admiration, curiosity and something akin to a yearning as if seeking a long-lost kindred spirit.

She was so used to people popping up and then disappearing she'd forgotten that the Platinum Stinger was there. "Dismissed." His hologram vanished and she refocused on the tactical displays to observe, like a well-oiled machine, the surviving ships in her fleet manoeuvring through the dense orbiting detritus to redeploy as she'd commanded.

They had only ever encountered their ships in space or their caterpillars on the ground - the most likely outcome from either scenario had been an arse-whipping. Not until the aliens had begun to set up shop on Omega Zero Three had they gained any understanding of the operations of these enormous ships. There was always the vague suggestion that their ships were composed of the strands but not in anyone's wildest dreams did they come up with strands made from the caterpillars. So, the enemy was modular in the extreme then. She punched up a real-time external visual as *Pantheon's* own railguns opened up ...

Clearly it took hundreds, if not thousands, of the columns to intertwine to make a single enemy ship. One well-timed railgun shot just as the columns were coalescing took them all out in one sitting. She nodded to herself: good to see that the gunnery officers were already ahead of her on this. She stayed with the external real-time for several minutes as the planet's high atmosphere began to look like it was being tormented by a multitude of mini suns bursting into life. As far as she could tell very few, if any at all, of the alien ships made it to orbit and her thermosphere retrieval was on the money.

She glanced up at readouts which confirmed that the vast majority of her Hoppers had already docked with their carriers. Refocusing on the real-time external view it took a couple of seconds for her to realise that there wasn't a malfunction with the projector; she was actually witnessing the entire planet starting to progressively fluctuate just like the alien ships did. Its colour was gradually changing from red to neon blue...

After about thirty seconds the planet slowly and most undramatically disintegrated - just like planetary formation in rapid reverse.

She didn't need to give any orders; all ships were putting distance between themselves and the gradually expanding sphere of rubble. There was a period of stunned silence and stillness in the Operations Centre followed by a burst of overexcited clamour. Above the commotion a few voices could clearly be heard.

"Somebody wanna tell me what the hell just happened!"

"Did we complete the lift?"

"Holy shit! Did you see that?!"

"Fuck! I've heard of scorched earth but..."

Three one-way holograms of her fellow Admirals simultaneously popped up in front of her. There was also a hologram of Vice Admiral Rahumaehullah, deputy to Admiral of the Fleet Susanna Choi-Tan. So, Susanna, one of very few people she'd call a friend, was dead. Although they were rarely on leave at the same time, they had been very close. She'd grieve later and prepare herself for the infinitely more onerous task of informing her husband that he'd lost his other wife.

Setting the tone of her voice she cut across the ferment, "All stations stay on it!" There was a moment of embarrassing silence then everyone in the OpsCen was heads-up, professionally getting back to their tasks. Just as instantly the four holograms vanished. "Press on! Do not allow them to break contact!"

With the inflating sphere of rubble that had been Omega Zero Three as the backdrop, the human ships like crazed wasps began chasing down the surviving alien ships. Launching frenzied missiles and railgun salvos they systematically set about whittling them down to nothing. Over the next hour or so a pattern emerged in this chaotic battle of absolute carnage - the surviving alien ships were, one by one, winking out of existence. Eventually there were no alien ships in view and the human ships amalgamated into formations that started sweeping back and forth across the solar system, hunting.

Chapter 10

All personnel had removed the helmets of their battle armour. There was a restrained air of relief and celebration. Admiral Akobundu-Tan sat deep in thought, resting her chin on her fist, staring off into nothingness. Currently, losses were at forty-seven percent; this would probably climb to fifty-three or, perhaps, fifty-four percent. That would still be the lowest of any engagement with the aliens, ever.

A detail contact report plus all electronic logs had already been sent to C 'n' C and she'd had an initial debrief with Field Martial Nagy and his command staff. No doubt every scrap of data was being pored over by the backroom boys seeking even the most minuscule competitive advantage that could be replicated and applied. There was already a hypothesis doing the rounds of how the aliens' weapons actually worked: neutralising or in some way negating the strong nuclear force in a defined area of matter and from a distance, resulting in atomic disintegration.

She wasn't inclined to give credence to mere speculation, but she could usually anticipate when her boss was about to give her bad news. Interrupting, when he began to wax lyrically about 'glorious victory' and 'civilian morale' she stated, categorically, that she had no intention of relinquishing her command to become a media gadfly or press the flesh with politicians. Then she cautioned that if he wanted her out of her OpsCen seat he'd need to dispatch the Provost Martial and his entire compliment of MPs to come get her. Field Martial Nagy laughed out loud. Always best to nip nonsense in the bud.

With her debriefing duties complete she refocused on the immediate. None of the four remaining rocky planets had surfaces or atmospheres suitable for ground ops and the Gas Giants between them didn't have a single respectable sized moon to speak of. This was paining her most of all: a solar system taken at such cost and for the first time besting the aliens but nowhere to put down a viable permanent base. She had her ship flying combat sweeps but deep down she knew that the enemy had already withdrawn and soon, after salvaging what she could, she'd need to pull out and regroup.

An automated stretcher with attached medical apparatus and accompanied by a nurse entered the Operations Centre. Akobundu-Tan sat up from her musing to stare at the Platinum Stinger. Still bedbound but definitely on the mend. Although he was no longer wearing dark goggles his eyes weren't back to normal. Not being one to shower motivational praise on her subordinates she still felt that what she had to say to this one individual, to whom they owed so much, needed to be said in person.

As the stretcher approached a Staff Officer turned to her. "It's the Field Martial, he's onboard *Hassock*, Ma'am."

Hooper's hologram appeared. *"You kicked arse, Admiral!"*

A sudden weariness overcame her. The post combat adrenalin run down she guessed. "That we did. But they have the capability of killing a planet, Laurent."

"Come on Ezocaagbo, you're the first to chalk up a clear victory."

"Maybe."

They had fought so many battles together. Her Land Forces Commander gave her a long assessing look before speaking. *"I heard about Susanna."*

She shrugged. She wasn't near ready to deal with that. She shrugged again.

"You worried about attaining their pain threshold?"

"Precisely. Have they gone for good or just to regroup?"

"*I suppose even prime number merchants recognise a tough nut when they see one.*"

"That's too logical, too comprehensible, too... human."

She found herself staring into Lume's eyes who was gazing apprehensively back at her: two Platinum Stingers sharing the same thought, '*They'll be back.*'

The End

PILOT

ISBN 978 0 9506087 6 7

The Explorer Corps' spaceship *Arabia* has the distinction of being the ship that has travelled the farthest distance from Earth. Eight days ago, Earth lost communication with the *Arabia*. The spacefighter, *Baddest*, is one of a pair of spaceships that, at more than fifty miles long are the largest machines ever built. *Baddest* is normally crewed by the Air Force's Ace Crew II but for this mission the crew is supplemented by the Navy's Special Combat Team Alpha. The Navy and Air Force are bitter space-borne rivals.

Mission: To find the vessel *Arabia* or to establish, beyond reasonable doubt, her fate and that of her crew.

EMPRESS

ISBN 978 0 9506087 4 3

She was the only one who could reunite the Empire and restore to its citizens the security that this brought. Without any doubt she was, singularly, the most important being alive. She and her cousin were the last of an Imperial bloodline. But her cousin could not easily supplant her. For Hial to sit on the Imperial throne she would need to be victorious in a bitter and bloody war. Such a war was to be avoided if at all possible.

Therefore, the primary task for Empress Morturina I, and those who served her, was to ensure her survival - at least until she had borne an heir to the Imperial throne.

All Woman

ISBN 978 0 9506087 2 9

There you are getting on with your life. When up pops THE blast from the past... The dim distant past - not seen, not heard of in eight years - but there he is. He's telling you the story: 'Sorry I dumped you, but having trashed all my subsequent relationships, I've finally come to realise that you are the one for me, we should be together.' It just so happens that he was the love of your life and it also happens that things are more than complicated...

What would you do?

INTERFACE

ISBN 978 0 9506087 4 7

It's the 80's. Clare is white, Patrick is black. They are from entirely different worlds, *but* when they met, they fell madly in love - perhaps opposites do attract. Now they plan to get married.
A straightforward proposition, right?

Well, maybe not. Set against them and their wishes are a host of 'interested parties': Clare's sister, Emma. Patrick's best friends, Harry and Nathan, and his ex-girlfriend, Otis. And of course, their parents want to have a say as well.

All the ingredients for a delightfully outrageous exploration of the *Interface* between: black men and white women; black men and black women; the maturity (or immaturity of men); strong personalities domination of weaker personalities.

Will love conquer all?

"There are many books written for women about the pregnancy and childbirth phenomenon. There doesn't seem to be much in this plethora of literature for men. It's about time there was!"- Ray A.

Thinking Man's Guide to Pregnancy, Childbirth & Fatherhood (ISBN 978 0 9526287 3 6) provides a male's tongue-in-cheek perspective of said phenomenon - a humorous slant on all things an expectant father needs to know but is too afraid to ask.

Disclaimer

Ray Anthony makes no claims to having any special qualifications for writing such a book, apart from having been there, seen it, and done it!

www.ingramcontent.com/pod-product-compliance
Lightning Source LLC
Chambersburg PA
CBHW061541050726
47593CB00002B/865